Humans, Being

A Story a Day for a Year

by Jimmy Doom

ISBN: 9798574607503
Edited by Dascha Paylor   dachapaylorauthor.com
Production Assistance by Coleen Parsons Novak
Cover Art by Brad Jendza   bradjendza.com
Layout/production by Tara Lingeman

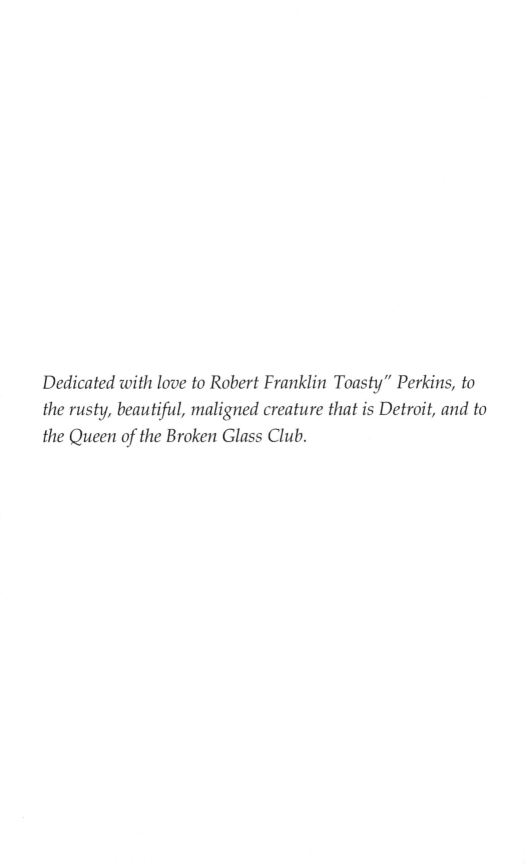

Dedicated with love to Robert Franklin Toasty" Perkins, to the rusty, beautiful, maligned creature that is Detroit, and to the Queen of the Broken Glass Club.

Author's Note:

Every story in this book is exactly 100 Words.

I started writing 100 Word Stories as a lark. Writer/Editor Rodney Goodall at *Micro Fictions* was the first person to cradle them to his bosom or at least begrudgingly publish them. Find Rodney at www.onequoteonestory.com.

Dascha Paylor took the microfiction baton and ran with it at *Tempest in Under 1000* which blossomed into

www.tempestwriters.com

I am deeply grateful to both those fine people for allowing me to spew my short musings to the world.

I did not invent the 100 Word Story, but those who seem to shepherd the work have a cute little nickname for the genre, and they also seem to have rules.

I don't mesh well with "cute" or with rules.

I hope you like the stories, and if you don't like them I hope you don't hesitate to tell me why;

the internet is overdue for its first argument.

Jimmy Doom

@JamesDoom

humansbeingbook@gmail.com

Reward

The woman, she was Janko's aunt, he found out, she was there again, outside the liquor store. The black and white photo of her lost Pomeranian was just above her black wool hat.

Last week, he had walked the alleys with her to look, calling, "Nani, Nani," with her and she made this kissing sound for Nani that gave him puke shivers.

The sign said "Reward" in black marker.

He had asked how much, and she said she didn't have much.

He gave her ten bucks toward the reward. He prayed with her.

But he was keeping the damn dog.

Leveling Up

She finished Level Seven for the first time about a mile from her bus stop. Ms. Balczyk was her least favorite teacher, but the word game she suggested fourth hour English try was exciting.

Level Eight had an added twist, and she was so engrossed she didn't just miss her stop, she accepted it and kept playing.

A man boarded the bus. He was grimy and smelly, and she was next to the only open seat. He sat down. She ignored him, playing Level Eight.

After a minute, the sketchy man said, "Syllablast! I just finished Level Eleven last night!

Locked & Loaded

Old Lou was sweeping out Rosseau's Barbers for what had to be the three thousandth time. Rosseau'd been trying to pay him for years. Rosseau's son would sneak money into Old Lou's coat, but Old Lou only wanted the bags of hair; he'd return the money.

The Rosseau's bought him a new coat for Christmas. After a bit of sleuthing, they found out he lived near the abandoned hospital. Makeshift shack.

As they neared, Mr. Rousseau marveled.

"He's got a chimney. There's two feet of snow on the roof. That, my boy, is the best hair-insulated house in the neighborhood."

Mourning, After

Larry was in the bathroom washing down aspirin with a mimosa, when Vivienne appeared in the mirror.

"You know you inherited the software business, right?"

Larry, juice and medicine in his mouth, just nodded.

"And that personal motto, the one you were reciting to the O'Hara's niece?"

Larry turned to face his wife, but only because there was nowhere to run.

"If that's your motto, I've never heard it in the twenty-four years we've been together.

And that thing about graduating at the top of your class?

Give me a break, Larry; you're an only child and you were homeschooled."

Fashion Statement

It was a bumpy bus ride. Conrad was thrilled Alex was behaving.

A drag queen boarded. She wore a tight green dress with a high, ruffled collar. The dress shimmered, like fish scales.

The drag queen had a five o'clock shadow.

Immediately Alex said, "Daddy, what's that?"

Conrad said, "Be polite."

Alex asked, "What's your name?"

The drag queen smiled. "I'm Vivika Del Mar."

"What do you do?" Alex asked.

"I make crowds scream with excitement."

Alex smiled. "I wanna make crowds excited like you!"

Vivika beamed.

Conrad said, "If you wanna do that at eighteen, I'll buy the dress."

Ned's Parking

Bobby's boss gave him the tickets last minute. He swung by The Blue Moon to pick up Jerry.

The windchill had dipped into the zeros, and the wind slapped Jerry hard as he jumped in the car.

They sped down to the arena, Jerry offering to pay for parking. He even had his wallet out as Bobby passed the Park and Lock.

"I'm paying," Jerry said. "Pull in."

"No way. Park and Lock. That's telling me what to do. It's my choice whether to lock the car or not. Infringement on my rights. We'll walk three blocks from Ned's Parking."

Needed

He picked weeds in the small park.

She grabbed her mail and thought that he looked like he needed a friend.

He walked to his mailbox. There was nothing. She saw this and knew that he needed a friend.

He stooped to pet the neighbor's dog, and the dog scurried from his reach.

She grabbed dough at the store to bake him some cookies.

She met the girls for brunch, blizzard be damned.

He shoveled snow. She heard the scraping. Then it stopped.

Later, she heard the sirens.

She sat on the porch in the cold and needed a friend.

Graceland

Larry McIntosh sat in his Elvis room, the car repossession letter on the Graceland replica coffee table he'd bought with a now canceled credit card.

His walking boot and his pistol were on top of the letter from the finance company.

His last five hundred, who was he kidding, five hundred he'd borrowed, was riding on the Cleveland Browns.

Tennessee scored. Larry popped some Percodans. Just like Elvis.

Tennessee scored again. Larry grabbed the pistol and shot his TV. Just like Elvis.

The bullet went through the flat screen, through the wall. The neighbor screamed.

Graceland was never an apartment.

Liquidation

After Paula bought the building, the former tenant showed her the panic button.

"Undesirables in the neighborhood" was the way they described it.

That implement of paranoia was the first thing she removed.

The people the former tenant thought were undesirable — they told her themselves they hadn't been welcome — became her helpers, her couriers, her advertising models.

Now out of business, boxes of vintage lace stockings and cinematic fedoras piled in the corner.

She couldn't cry over business. She might cry over people. And when she saw Henry, in silhouette, diligently washing the windows of an empty storefront, she did.

Personality Crisis

"How are your kids doing?"

Foster chuckled.

"The oldest wishes real life was Grand Theft Auto. No arrests that I know of, but it won't shock me.

"The youngest wants to teach Constitutional Law, but only if they throw out everything but the Second Amendment. She'll be the one to break the oldest out of prison.

"And the middle one is a mix of the other two; Very much into the Bible, but only the parts with the slavery, the rebellion and the sex."

"You happy with your decision to not have kids?"

Andrea smiled at Foster. "I am now."

Piano Man

The piano player at the last bar before the freeway was such a drunk, sometimes they called him Liver-racci to his face. He had a tip jar instead of a candelabra.

Leslie warned Mike that the guy was a bad piano player, but the bar poured stiff cheap drinks.

After five of 'em, Mike approached the piano.

"Mind if I play a song for my lady?"

Liveracci, gin oozing from his pores, looked at Mike.

"You can't play piano with one hand, son."

Mike grabbed his loafer with his prosthetic arm.

"Really, asshole?" he said to Liveracci. "Hold my shoe."

Pregnant

Klimczyk slid into the booth across from Bernard.

"Climax! Good to see ya," Bernard yelled, already boozy.

"Don't call me that, Bern. Ever again."

Bernard straightened.

"You're gonna retire your infamous nickname?"

Klimczyk grabbed his friend by the shoulders.

"Come outside and punch me. Beat me up. Let's get it over with.

Bernard burped.

"Did someone dust you at Hines Park? You are acting insane."

Klimczyk walked out and Bernard followed.

Klimczyk bowed his head.

"I got your sister pregnant."

"Holy shit, Climax, you got Cheryl pregnant?"

"No, Bern, not Cheryl. Mary Beth. I got Mary Beth pregnant."

Bernard swung.

Moths

We sobered up together, mostly. A few smuggled in half pints and flasks. The place was called The Lantern. The after-bar crowd was the moths. Walk in drunk and walk out full and sleepy.

The girl with the haunted eyes wrote poetry in the corner booth. The scene was cinematic and felt sad, like she should have been at the bar with us having fun instead of scribbling alone, waiting for us to disturb her, flirt with her. The little diner is gone now. The poem she gave me is lost, but the bar is still there, and always packed.

Proud Momma

McIntyre avoids going to his mom's house. He doesn't dislike her, but the newspaper articles about his burning car heroics are framed, in the middle of the living room. It was twenty-four years ago. He stopped getting a Christmas card from the kid he saved about seven years ago.

But what's she supposed to be proud of? His wedding band? He makes money from it but…

He uses his spare key to unlock her door. Her hearing's been gone for a while.

She's asleep on the sofa right under the framed page three story.

McIntyre realizes she's not just asleep.

Getting Hotter

Quickies in the walk-in at Pastapalooza morphed into dating. The second date, Carrie found herself waiting in line at the mall for Ephraim to get a bottle of hot sauce signed by celebrity chef Basil Braunstein.

They sweated as the line crawled, and Carrie's patience waned.

Realizing they would be waiting for another hour, she yanked Ephraim out of line as he stammered a protest.

"I have a better surprise," she said.

"Better than meeting the maker of the planet's best hot sauce?"

Carrie nodded. "We're going to the *mi Abuela s*. She makes the best. Better yet, she'll teach you how."

Quality Time

Allison blew through red lights getting to the hospital. George's voicemail was vague, but he did say, "Everyone's alive."

George was standing outside Emergency pacing, vaping when Allison arrived.

Allison almost slipped on the ice getting out of the car. George met her halfway.

"Your dad had a heart attack."

"Tristan was supposed to shovel the snow!"

Allison ran past George toward the entrance.

"Tristan did shovel his snow, honey."

"Then how? And where is Tristan?"

"He's in there too, sedated."

Allison screamed, "What???"

"He feels responsible. After he got done shoveling, he talked Grandpa into a video game marathon."

Radar

Narinna sat in the booth at the restaurant and listened to Betsy lie to Ryan for a half hour.

When they got in the car, Narinna said, "I was sitting right there. You know I know it was all lies. Talk to me. Why?"

Betsy smiled.

"I've got this thing called the internet. He sounded too good to be true, so I looked him up. Didn't graduate from Dartmouth, none of that. He's been lying to you. I could have warned you, but I decided to handle it my own way. Don't play matchmaker anymore, okay? Your radar isn't calibrated."

Life Spans

Handing his nephew his birthday gift card, George asked, "What does my favorite nineteen-year-old do with his time?"

Ray said, "I put some small hunks of chicken in my gym in the garage. Been working on my martial arts reflexes catching flies barehand."

George grunted. "Common house flies only live about two weeks and you're torturing the damn things."

Ray said, "I'm trying to better myself."

George put his hand on Ray's shoulder.

"Lots of kids your age are down at the fountain every day protesting police brutality and inequality. And the old, racist motherfuckers seem like they live forever."

Receipt

She noticed her receipt from the new bagel place said, "Cute Girl in Hat."

It had been a gift, it was warm, but she hated it.

Apparently, she looked cute in it to someone at the bagel place. She wore it the next visit.

The receipt: "Cute Girl in Hat." She smiled.

The next week, it said, "Girl in Hat." Her disappointment bit into her. The following week she left the hat home.

Her receipt said, "Margot Robbie lookalike." She flushed and giggled.

A woman's voice said, "Miss, you have the wrong order."

She went home and discarded the hat.

Reentry

"Hey, Dave, thanks for answering. I'm out. Sixty days. It was wild, emotional. I know I have some apologizing to do…"

Dave had been to rehab before. He reached deep into a personal well of sympathy to find a drop of it. He also had to hold back from throwing his phone against the kitchen wall.

"I'm probably never going to accept your apology, Marc. You should probably spend your energy elsewhere. June is pregnant. She's keeping it. It's not mine. I'm going to assume it's yours, based on what she told me. Good Luck. One Day at a Time."

Mama Knows Best

Tony answered, "Yello," like he always did.

Nick was laughing before he could form words.

"Tone, remember when Mama promised us if she lived to be eighty, she'd get a tattoo?"

Tony snorted humorlessly.

"You call me at one in the morning on Sunday to talk about Mama and the stupid tattoo thing?"

Nick laughed louder.

"Tone, maybe she'll get it in prison."

"The hell you talkin 'about Nicky?"

"I'm at the precinct. Mama's getting charged with breaking and entering."

Tony whistled. "You're serious?"

"Yeah, Tony. She broke into Bonomosso's to prove once and for all they freeze their cannelloni."

Lyrics

The record store owner recommended the band.

She was so enthusiastic Donnie couldn't say no.

It was weeks before he spun the vinyl, then not a day went by that he didn't.

The groove, the guitar tone, everything was in his musical Eden.

And the lyrics: intelligent, thoughtful, poetic.

The opening line to the song, Occlusion, was his new rallying cry.

Seven months later they came to town.

Bella, the record store owner, got Donnie backstage.

He proudly showed Ian, the singer, the tattoo of the lyrics.

Ian autographed the record, unable to tell Donnie he had misheard the words.

Lunch Counter Blues

Barry felt like he had stuffed a stained chiffon dress between his legs.

Ajit picked up on his friend's discomfort immediately.

"Don't tell me something's wrong with your coney."

"Hell no," Barry said, "these are the finest foodstuffs known to man."

"You didn't look happy."

Barry lifted the metal canister of napkins.

"Every time we're here, we go through hundreds of these flimsy little folded excuses for a napkin. I'm trying to figure out how much thicker and more absorbent they would have to make them to save paper. It's counterintuitive."

Ajit snorted. "It's not the chili causing your ulcer."

Room with a View

It was date number two, a little Italian place by the zoo.

"I've told you so much about my work and my pets," Denise said.

"What about you? Any interesting or unique hobbies?"

Nate smiled, sipped wine, took a moment.

"My father used to ridicule me for having a smaller than average penis," he said, "so when I'm standing at a line of urinals I look at other men's penises. Not in a sexual way, mind you, but because I need to reassure myself that I'm not that small."

"Oh…" Denise composed herself and smiled. "Anything else?"

Nate nodded. "Boxing."

Rotten

The antique chair splintered when his father hit the ground. The chair was the only thing Denny would feel bad about later.

Before his father could struggle to his feet, Denny had the old man's twelve gauge. He considered putting it in his trunk while his father thought about why he got hit.

It was a real punch, a sucker punch, truthfully.

But his father had shot at kids for stealing peaches off his tree. Denny knew it was principle, not peaches because every year, when Denny visited for the old man's birthday, the fruit was rotting on the tree.

Sanguine

McNaughton and Baum walked out of the call center, Baum seriously concerned for his friend.

"Evans meant what he said about hangovers, Mick; I can tell. You gonna quit drinking on work nights?"

The question was answered at bowling, when McNaughton ordered a double Chambord.

"Not a great idea, Mick. It's the only call center gig in the county." Baum picked his ball from the rack.

"There's something primal about red liquid, Bomber. If this is gonna be my last drink, I want it to feel like the blood of Christ."

Baum spun. "Hippie coffeehouse next door serves hibiscus tea."

No Youth   Sean Nader

Action Figures

"I feel like we're three-chording our way toward extinction," Maple said, foam indeterminate hanging from their lip.

"We've been a bobsled on a torture highway since twenty-seven arbitrarily became the rock n roll horse latitude."

The bridge swayed slightly, triggering Kelly's vertigo.

"Sing that in the park, Maple, not here with the cops on their way and me too upset to remember it later."

Maple spit.

"Just once I wanna go to someone's house and see their action figures off the shelf, see them on the floor with 'em, fighting each other, breaking plastic, like the world does to us."

Inspired by the art of Sean Nader

Shift Change

The server brought the cannoli.

Allison took a bite.

"I saw the texts you sent to Sara."

Robert cleared his throat.

"The one inviting her to the basketball game you couldn't go to?"

"Plural, Robert. All of them. I hope."

He bristled.

"You invited me out to dinner to tell me this? To our favorite spot?"

"Yes. You go out for a damn smoke every time we're here. When you do, a server always tells me I'm the most beautiful woman he's ever seen."

"That's unprofessional."

"It's sweet. When his shift is over, we're going on a date. Goodbye, Robert."

Slumber Cinema

The hot sauce had stained the rice red when Mathilde Prescott walked into the kitchen.

"Frederick, it's after midnight. You can't eat that! Spicy food gives you foul dreams!"

Frederick turned, spoon overflowing with sodden rice almost to his lips.

"Mother, I am thirty-two years old. I live with my parents in a tiny condo in a town where a grease fire at the Dairy Nozzle is headline news. I can't pleasure myself with abandon because either you or Father is always here.

"I am no longer eating bland foods. Engineering my own nightmares is the only excitement I have."

Survived By

Beckley walked with some haste toward his boss.

Checking to make sure no mourners were in earshot, he whispered, "A whole year I've been working here and the guy in the Evergreen Room is giving far and away the weirdest eulogy. It's all gibberish, like he's having a stroke."

Charles motioned for Beckley to follow him and proceeded to the door adjacent the small service.

He listened briefly, smiled, then had Beckley follow him to the office, shutting the door.

"You need to get to know the clients better, Son. The deceased was president of the Lewis Carroll Fan Club."

The Favor

Kathryn Whitlock was thrilled when Bart's dad answered the door.

"Hi, Mr. Felson. Came here to ask a favor."

Felson smiled. "Anything, Kathryn. Bart loves you."

"That's the problem. He's infatuated. It was flattering, but it's not reciprocal."

"Give him a chance, sweetheart, he's…"

Kathryn folded her arms, inhaled. "I told him I wasn't interested. My decision's final. He wasn't raised to respect women, Mr. Felson."

Felson stammered to object.

"Sorry, Mr. Felson, it's true."

Bart's Dad nodded, chastened.

"What should I say?"

"Tell him women aren't game animals to be hunted," she said. "Tell him

trophies are for bowling."

Magic Formula

The guy stood, scowling, pulling on his coat, breathing through clenched teeth and pursed lips.

"This bar pours lousy drinks," he said to Wesley, or to no one.

Wesley drummed his fingers on the bar.

"No, the bar doesn't pour weak drinks. You walked in, asked if there were daily specials, didn't tip the bartender on the first round. When she didn't respond to your cliched flirtations, you asked her if her boyfriend was in the band 'or something. 'Who her partner is, is none of your business and whether you know it or not, you begged for weak drinks."

Starving

Aren't you a much better artist, now that you're hungry?

The donkey is much cuter chasing the dangling carrot that he used to be allowed to nibble every few miles, but now must stare at until dusk.

His master repeatedly tells him how much he loves him but shows him none.

The master reminds him how beautiful the valley is but won't remove the donkey's blinders.

The master only touches the donkey's flesh in a brief stroke before pushing him forward.

A woman calls to the master.

"What is your donkey's name?"

"He has no name. My name is Mejeum."

Out of the Bottle

Yvette finished Ed's bottle of gin. Now she regretted it in the mirror.

Usually, the kids drew on her when she passed out. This time, they shaved her eyebrows and part of her head.

She did a shot of mouthwash and found Hillary in front of the computer.

Hilary was grinning like she got straight A's.

"Not funny with the dog clippers, Hill. I was gonna apply for jobs today."

Hillary smiled even more broadly.

"You have a job, mom. Your job is pretending to have cancer. I started a GoFundMe with the pictures. We're up to three thousand already."

The Bell and the Owl

The recessed doorway of the vacant shop felt like a sauna compared to the chilling wind out on the darkening dead-end street.

Braylon Humphries tucked his feet under his ass for extra warmth. As he did, a deep, percussive note sounded. In his startled state, he flinched, and his left leg cramped fiercely.

Across the way, the Eurasian owl that was the bookstore mascot stared at him unsympathetically.

His luck, generally bad, seemed to be deteriorating until he realized that the note he heard was the church bell, and the priest was always willing to share cigarettes and a meal.

The Four Seasons

It not only seemed to be a reasonable expectation, it seemed to be something easy for the hotel to accomplish: he wanted a room on one of the bottom two floors because he was afraid of heights.

But someone had recognized his name and assumed the low room was an error.

Now he had a room twenty-seven stories above an empty beach he was afraid to look down upon. The lake was almost frozen over. The hills were snow-covered.

He wasn't afraid of speed. He called the concierge and asked for a case of champagne, two escorts, and a toboggan.

Would

The smoke wafted through the small room.

"This will chase away bad energies in your apartment, Grandma."

Quesha waited for the embers to smolder and set the Palo Santo on a small coaster.

Grandma sipped her beer, cackling. "Ain't no such thing as magic wood."

"I'll check back," Quesha told her.

"At least it smells good," Grandma said.

Quesha called in a week. "How you feeling, Grandma?"

"Never been better," Grandma answered.

"Palo Santo works!" Quesha'd believed it all along.

"I don't believe that nonsense," Grandma said, "but my dashing neighbor gentleman stopped by to compliment me on my incense."

Alphabet

Danny stared.

After seventeen years together, looking at her hadn't lost the Disneyland.

Danny listened.

His wife was now famous. She gave the best interviews ever. Not just among her chef peers. Of any celebrity Danny knew. His love and pride cascaded from him.

The interviewer asked what she cooked for her husband.

It was like a car going under a bridge. The radio went silent.

Nothing.

Then: "I'd like to keep that secret."

Danny wished she would say Alphabet soup. They would sit on each other's laps, spelling letters. It was romantic.

Instead, she lied. "He cooks for me."

James Dean

The credits rolled on Giant. Fortier cracked his knuckles, living in a permanent daydream.

He brushed past the sports clippings, framed, faded.

He grabbed his keys.

The small brass tag said, "Employee of the Year."

His mom had his homecoming king photo on the nightstand at assisted living.

He should visit, but he didn't.

James Dean would be eighty-nine today.

He coulda been James Dean, Fortier told himself.

He always told himself that.

His father's favorite word was "paycheck" and he cowardly followed that path.

James Dean would have been 89.

Fortier drove fast to visit his mother after all.

Invitation Only

He'd stopped using animals in his theme parties, but Chester was still the master of the raucous, "night you'll never forget even if you don't entirely remember" soirees.

This one was a celebration of front liners: nurses, firefighters, grocery store employees.

He made IVs full of neon cocktails, hors d'oeuvres that rolled by on a grocery conveyor, sirens every hour that signaled everyone to remove an article of clothing.

He woke in his loft the next morning to fire in his bedroom. A naked man ran around the corner and sprayed the flames with a fire extinguisher full of confetti.

Word Woes

The complaints hadn't stopped for hours, but the drinks hadn't stopped either. It was a rather pro piece of bar etiquette. The liquid stranger knew, from experience, that someone would listen if the vodka lubed the conversation.

His complaints were mundane, and nearly universal: money, infidelity, and lack of appreciation.

In the bar mirror, Ed could see his own chicken pox scar, but not the deep grooves where his uncle had taken out his eye with a salad fork.

"Ya know what I mean?" The stranger said.

"I know what you're saying," Ed said, "but I don't share your woes."

Airmail

There are different ways of being a prisoner but there are a million ways to break out of jail. Arlene had to remember that. She was her own boss now but couldn't forget working at Amalgamated Dynamo.

Hum Wagner all day long, didn't matter: she still heard the machines echo in her head.

She couldn't let bad memories dog her. She was too smart. She had to move forward.

The package would do no good sitting in her front seat.

Forget the past, she thought, forget the bad luck, the inter-office conspiracy.

She dropped her patent application in the mailbox.

Mirage

Welch was at a *food* or *roof* decision. His hunger was tangible.

Plummeting temperatures were cheering for "roof." The smells of the nearby restaurants were shouting the other way.

He thought he saw a samosa on a napkin on the ground.

People discarded food constantly.

He bent until he realized that the napkin was real, but the samosa was a brown leaf.

He thought of his father, who hated their neighborhood's immigrants. Had the immigrants not come, Welch wouldn't have even known what a samosa was. His father wouldn't touch foreign cuisine, but Welch would dream of it all night.

Scratch

She was explaining the difference between arachnid and insect. My bladder went from petulant to demanding.

Scratched in the wood above the urinal, not too far above, dangerously close to pissable, were the words TK loves MB.

I would never love the woman I was with tonight. This was looking like a handshake goodnight.

Who scratches their heartfelt emotions near urinals? How well did TK know MB?

The scratches were thick, deep. They had been painted over, twice, at least. TK Loves MB was naked, raw wood.

TK was a regular. I didn't know. But I believed he loved MB.

The Empress

She bid farewell to her third love-desperate, relationship-seeking client in a row.

Sasha loved her job. She truly felt the gift of being intuitive. She appreciated being paid for it, but some days the loneliness cascaded through the door of the little suburban flea market.

They were mostly women: articulate, pretty in their own way…

But Sasha wanted to say to some, "Brush your teeth." "Quit bragging about your degrees; men don't care."

Then a new male client walked in, looking for a soulmate.

Sasha gave herself cramps suppressing a laugh, wishing she could sell the man her client list.

Critical

The boxes had water stains; there were dead moths stuck to some clothes.

But her father's music collection had survived the years of neglect and basement floods, and Claudine was thrilled to digitize it all, alphabetically. She uploaded through B before some unlabeled cassettes in a musty box set her curiosity on fire.

The songs were live, there were glasses clinking, the vocals were muffled, the guitar player was awful.

She called her dad.

"There's some live stuff on cassettes, no label, awful guitar player. Know who it is?"

Claudine's dad said, "If the guitar's really bad, that's your mom."

Just Add Milk

Kelly called her mom.

"Mom, I need to tell you something; you're going to be upset. I want you to know everyone's fine…but…"

"But what?" Kelly's mom said, panicking.

"We slept late after the trip. Dennis gets his own breakfast almost always anyway. Ya know that little blue alien cereal mascot he likes so much?"

"He didn't choke on a toy, did he?" Kelly's mom almost hyperventilated.

"No, Mom. He got ahold of Mike's tattoo equipment and tattooed the alien on himself. I know he's only eleven years old...but it looks exactly like the one on the box."

Vertigo

"It was a great idea. Really. Logical. Wonderful."

The words were supposed to comfort, but Mark's voice was maudlin.

The festive Blue Margarita was the absolute wrong choice. Evan pushed it aside.

"Elevation was the natural progression," he said, more angry than sad.

"Everyone in the office agreed, Evan. They couldn't wait to give you a development team."

"And we slapped warnings all over the damn thing!" Evan nearly yelled.

Mark glanced up at the television behind the resort bar.

Even with his limited Spanish, he knew what the crawl said: "Rock Climbing Fitness App Blamed in Dozens of Deaths."

Watching

Frank resisted the nanny-cams. But Anita insisted.

Frank hadn't really argued, so much as presented a list of things he didn't believe.

The baby is so young; nothing bad can happen.

We can't really afford them.

It's an invasion of her privacy.

Anita won; they installed the cams. Her post-partum funk seemed to have lifted.

They planned a cottage getaway, the first since the birth of Bryson.

Frank would go open the cottage. Anita would meet him Friday evening.

She surprised him Thursday night, as he sat pleasuring himself to live video of the nanny, fully clothed, doing the dishes.

Ditch

Christine was to the point that she felt like her cubicle was swallowing her personality.

But her job was safe, her industry secure.

Ironic, then, that she was risking her life on an icy freeway to get there.

If she slid into a ditch and wrecked her car, would it be worth it?

Or was her cubicle a ditch, and her life slid in there every day?

The map app showed dozens of hazards and crashes.

She jerked the wheel to the right.

The car spun off.

She got out.

Surveyed the damage.

She did not call in to work.

Grandma Said

Bertie sat down next to his grandfather.

"Grandpop, Grandma said you were the best football player in the history of the state."

Mickey shook his head. "Your Grandma loves me, and that's not exactly true."

"Grandpop," Bertie said, "Grandma says you were in the war. Tell me about it."

Mickey looked at his grandson.

"War isn't good conversation, pal. Ever."

Bertie grimaced.

"Grandpop, Grandma said you used to work at haunted houses, playing one of the scary monsters that made people scream."

Mickey smiled. "Go tell your grandma you're staying up past your bedtime and get me a storytellin 'beer."

Full of Grace

Using dating apps felt like a failure, but Rhonda was determined to be smart.

She wore a rosary she inherited from her aunt. If the guy in real life didn't live up to the profile, she fondled it, explaining how she wasn't going to have sex until marriage due to her religious beliefs.

She had used it twice on dates that ended quickly. Twice it had ended up on a bedroom floor.

She deployed it at a cafe near the river, pulling it from underneath her sweater, and Becker, the retirement planner, began with reverence, to recite the Hail Mary.

Anthropomorphic

Jeffrey kicked his head back, banging the locker. He was still wearing the top of the anthropomorphic Blizzard.

End of season, end of job. His bum ankle throbbed; his agent was retiring; tonight he'd collect his last game check.

He kept telling himself a mascot was more than an actor, kept not believing it.

He slipped the head off.

The backup goalie, the hot one, the one who always got booed, walked past, backed up.

"Join us for drinks at Max's?"

Jeffrey put the head back on.

"Fuck yes!" he said," adding, "I always wanted to swear in this costume."

Tough Love

Miller had been singin 'on the streetcorner since he got outta rehab.

Metz, who owned the sub shop loved him, fed him, even brought him to his fourth of July barbecue.

Borgo, who owned the record shop gave him soul records and a working turntable.

Lady at the bakery gave him a kitten.

Theresa from the coffee place always got his smokes.

She was coming toward him now.

"Hey sweet child, you mind grabbin'…"

"Oh, hell no," she said.

"My mom was watching you sing last night. You coughed up blood after My Cherie Amour. No more smokes for you."

Celebrity

It was over an hour's drive from where he lived.

He inflated the leaking tire and went.

It was a below-average self-service car wash. The dirty Grand Opening sign certainly had been used at other grand openings.

The old motorcycle racer was there, signing autographs. The line was short.

He'd beaten his wife, shot a kid in the face, done seventeen years.

But he was a celebrity.

Emory waited his turn.

"My dad is your third cousin," he said. "Named me after you."

"That's beautiful," the racer said.

Emory pulled the gun. "You're gonna pay so I can change it."

Long Ride

Lathan did lots of mescaline at twelve. That was on his psyche report, still, released after twenty years.

A woman walked into the office, beautiful, though all women were after twenty years inside.

"We know each other, Mr. Emmett," she said. "I want you to know, first and foremost: I forgive you."

"OK," Lathan said, confused.

Then the glimmer of recognition sparked.

"Fuck me! You're Parker's little sister. I threw your bike off the roof of your house because you wouldn't kiss me."

"I'm your P.O.," she said. "I could have recused myself, but your childhood behavior's why I'm here."

Boxes and Rings

Her perk, for living in the house behind the liquor store, was that she consistently had access to boxes when her peripatetic friends moved.

The downfalls were the rats, the groups of giggling teenagers sucking on Whip-its, discarding the gas canisters, shotgunning cans of beer, flipping the plastic six-pack rings, destined to someday, somewhere, choke a bird to death.

Knowing the kids wouldn't listen if she complained, she collected the plastic rings, even fashioning herself a homemade fire escape.

While her friends moved on and up, she realized she must stay, because no one else would clean up party alley.

Display

Vince called. Sweat was dripping off his voice.

"Markus, you won't believe this. Some agency's at Mom's house and she's about to film a commercial for you know who."

Markus didn't agree with his Mom's political stance, but he never thought she'd get enamored enough of this guy to agree to a commercial.

He sped to her townhouse.

There she was, underneath a bright light, Markus's military medals and commendations in the background.

He walked in past the crew, kissed his mother on the forehead, lifted the frame with his Bronze Star off the wall and stepped to the side.

Compatible

The channels flipped by, Paco getting tired of having no good live sports on during the pandemic.

Cordell was in the kitchen tapping away at his laptop.

"The hell you working on?" Paco asked.

"Dating profile. They match you based on thirty-three categories. It's complicated."

"Get a dog," Paco said.

"Shutup."

"I'm serious," Paco insisted. "You know you're a match for a dog in four important categories. All humans and dogs have them in common."

Cordell stood, annoyed.

"Yeah, what are they?"

Paco gave Cordell his serious look.

"Dogs and humans both like walks, playing catch, naps, and peanut butter."

Out

He was one tantrum away from the booking agent dropping him forever.

He was fine with that, really.

The rooms were less full. The hit, which only treaded Number One chart water before drowning in a sea of pablum pop country, was more novelty than beloved.

Singing the word "she" caught in his throat like a plastic sword impaling a martini olive.

He kicked his guitar across the theater stage and found the production office and his manager Vic.

"I want out," he said.

"Out?" Vic asked. "Out of the contract?"

"Out of the contract, and out of the closet."

Painting

The boys played with their toy trucks on the kitchen floor. Lights from the house next door illuminated their play area.

The new people were moved in. The abandoned house was a palace.

Dad explained "gentrification".

There was music next door. Mellow jazz. The boys played.

A woman's scream. The boys had played in the home when it was abandoned. It felt like theirs. They ran to help the woman.

There was no intruder. No blood. A mover had torn an oil painting. The woman sobbed.

The boys were in a whole new neighborhood, never having moved from their own.

Passion Play

Larry was cringing while waiting for Marisa to answer. He had to know the reason for the silence.

"Hello," she said, disinterest dripping from her voice. She had to know it was him. Programmed into her phone might be as deep as their relationship would go.

"You don't answer texts," he said.

"Because either your vocabulary or your priorities are horrible," Marisa responded, cold but measured. "Not just your texts, but your personal profile. It says *Passionate about paid advertisements.* If you're passionate about them in a world full of oppression, you're shallow. If you think that's passion, you're dumb."

Perch

Cars zipped past when the light was green, but Armando didn't care. He danced and flipped in the fish costume that he and Aunt Georgia had made themselves.

When the light was red, he danced into the street until the cops made him stop.

When Georgia's Pride Perch Sammiches opened a new location, she even paid him.

Armando performed at all the openings, then on the commercials.

He and Georgia cried happy tears when she sold the company for millions.

He cried again when the new commercial aired. A comedian he couldn't stand was playing a perch he didn't recognize.

Piñata

"I feel like a piñata, totally poked with needles."

Mary stirred her martini before responding.

"Typically, piñatas are struck with a large stick by a blindfolded child at a birthday celebration. In your case, experts keep drawing blood to determine what's wrong with you. Physically, I mean."

Anthony sighed, frustrated.

"You're not being very supportive," he said.

Mary popped an anchovy olive into her mouth.

Before she fully swallowed, she replied, "Seeing as your mystery illness might be the result of your repeated dalliances with women outside our vows, I'd say the health coverage my employer provides constitutes fantastic support."

Quarantine

Technology was going to keep order during the quarantine, Rogers was certain.

Not just medical technology, but streaming services, multiplayer gaming, and the online state lottery system he and Rebecca were doing a maintenance diagnostic on now.

The State Commission chairman was distracted on his phone.

Rebecca said, "Rogers, do you know you just cleared the probability algorithm override?"

Rogers pinched her arm.

She glared at him.

"I need you to back me up," he whispered.

"But that means…" she began.

"The entire state is gonna be locked in their houses," Rogers said. "Let's give them something to smile about."

Reckoning

Karoline took one last swig of wine before she spoke. "You don't miss Trevor, do you?"

Anita looked shocked, then dropped the facade.

"He shot at the cops before they shot him."

"He was your son, Anita. You played the grieving mother very well when it served you."

Anita tried to interject, but Karoline had the stage.

"When you liked Billy Freed in high school, you left a sweater at his parent's restaurant. You sobbed. I remember thinking that it wasn't for the absence of, or the desire for the sweater, it was for your embarrassment at leaving it behind."

Recliner

Cigars were part of the charm when Stevie was eight.
Jumping on Grampa's lap on that ratty recliner, inches from
the hots of that stogie.

At thirteen, puberty, Katie wouldn't sit with him because he
smelled of cigars. He stopped going to see Grampa so often.

When he did, he hated the sight and smell of the bloated old
man, scotch and smoke.

Steve helped moved his Grampa into assisted living.

"Take the recliner," Grampa said.

"I think I'm gonna toss it, Gramps."

"There's four grand stuffed in the leg rest. Take it to the casino.
Put it on red."

Recommendation

"Vicki knows a guy."

Haas scratched his armpit, way too close to Rhonda's fries.

"What does Vicki know about cement?" Haas asked, as if he had already answered his own question with "nothing."

Rhonda answered. "Her and Blake are very happy with his work, and he was a few grand less than the nearest competitor.

Haas scratched his pit again, then ate a fry off Rhonda's plate.

"Get an estimate," Haas said.

"ASAP," Rhonda said. "I promise."

Vicki's cement guy did a marvelous job, Rhonda thought. The cement work was affordable. Burying Haas underneath it had been a bit pricey.

Reflection

Kittle put the damn poster in the writing room to inspire himself. The Clash, London Calling. But the frame is glass, and glass reflects the tattoo, the ridiculous portrait tattoo.

What relationship lasts forever? He's supposed to be a writer; he knows that's not plausible.

Writing on a typewriter because, if he was on a computer, he would stalk her friends on social media.

Editing in pen because, if he had liquid paper, he'd huff it.

Write the damn novel, Kittle; prove you're worthy of her, he tells himself before he smashes the poster glass and quits for the night.

Retirement

After Wally's funeral, Lanie moved to their cottage in Glen Arbor.

Tennis held no luster for her without him; she impulsively sold her skates at their last garage sale.

She decided to be the last person on earth to spend time on the internet.

There really were wondrous things to see and buy. Mostly buy.

Overnight delivery! What a concept.

Someone pulled into the gravel driveway. The girls! A surprise visit, damn them!

She hid some wine bottles, shoved socks in silverware drawers…

But the first thing they saw, on the table, was the thousand-piece jigsaw puzzle of Wally naked.

Rush Hour

Lightning flashed. He saw a brown blur dance from a Toyota bumper.

At a full stop on the four lane when his brain processed

"Airedale mix."

The dog darted against the traffic flow.

Rickard got out of his car. Kinda stupid. The guy behind him was already honking.

Rickard pointed in the vicinity of the dog. More honks. Brakes squealing, the radio static hiss of wet pavement.

The honking guy behind Rickard got out of his car.

Crash. Metal on metal. Rickard cringed. But here came the Airedale, galloping.

Honking guy crouched, holding a steak. All the cars had stopped.

Shaded

Rita hated math but other than that loved helping Timmy with homework. He was struggling in some classes. She didn't want him to be ineligible for lacrosse.

She sat down as he was turning on his school tablet, and the word GOWLD appeared on the screen. She'd seen it before. On a viaduct, huge letters.

"Gowld? That's not a gang, is it?"

Timmy laughed.

"No, Mom, not a gang."

"Is it a band or rapper or something?" She asked.

Timmy laughed harder. "I wish. It's our name, silly."

"Our name is Gold."

"On the streets, Mom, I add a W."

Shadows

His father had been a funny weatherman, beloved throughout their Midwest college town.

Rodney knew his father wanted him to pursue broadcasting. His father's world of joking about barometric pressure had given the family a comfortable life.

Rodney was unable to conquer a stutter to achieve a broadcasting career.

He sat in the family's cavernous home listening to a police scanner.

He began to show up at robberies and bus fires, teachers strikes and random vandalism.

Sometimes he would introduce himself to crime victims after the cameras left.

Sometimes they would recognize his name and speak fondly of his father.

Screeching Halt

He was shorter in person than Muriel thought he'd be but truly handsome.

Scott said, "Let's get a picture with him."

Muriel whispered, "Leave him alone. He's attending to personal business, give him his privacy."

Scott stood, pulling his phone from his pocket.

"Jesus Christ, Muriel, he's at a brake shop, not a funeral parlor!"

Ryan Vagner turned and looked at the couple.

Scott beamed.

"Ryan, we love your movies! How about a picture with us?"

Muriel's neck tingled. She remembered an interview…

The movie star shook his head.

No.

"I will not take a photo with anyone who blasphemes."

Untitled   **Bumbo Brian Krawczyk**

Performance

Everything in life is performance.

Armand, standing at the mirror, going through his stage fright ritual.

Bertrand, doing ridiculous yoga poses as he plays uber agent while Armand frets.

Armand is Bertrand's only client, his rare others, grown tired of his shenanigans, have moved on.

And I, the dutiful assistant, stroking Armand's ego, keeping Armand's secrets, lustily applauding for songs I've heard thousands of times.

My performance is the deftest.

Because Bertrand made Armand a rich man, and Armand needs his ritual to perform.

I love Armand but never let on that I want to sing those words to him.

Inspired by the art of Brian "Bumbo" Krawczyk

Permission

Miranda stroked the fur with two fingers, almost blanketing the small body…

"Extraordinary that school would assume a family would allow a rodent at home."

"I won her, mother. For an essay. On responsibility for living things."

"You have a responsibility to me to not bring unwanted creatures into my domicile."

"Veronica won't leave her cage, mother."

"You've given it a name? How impulsive."

Miranda's mother snatched the cage from the dresser and strode toward the bathroom.

Miranda heard the flush.

Her mother returned, handing her the empty cage.

"Return this to school."

"May I have permission to cry, Mother?"

Soft Cover

The wood floors were murder on her knees, but the books had to be boxed and the pillows were already packed.

She left the books for last, purposely, lying to herself that she would leave some behind for the new tenant.

They were all paperbacks because that's all she'd been able to afford.

They were dog eared because she had gotten lost in them and hadn't cared.

Her debut novel was a success. She could afford to pay someone to do this. She could afford hardcovers of all of these, but the books were her friends when she was nobody.

Stars

He loved space as a little boy. The stars, the limitless possibilities. His space wasn't one of rayguns, and wars, but one of peace and solitude.

In the summer he ripped the sheet metal roof off his hut near the viaduct and just stared at the stars.

He endured the rain for his quality time with the billions of twinkling lights that couldn't be drowned by the noise of the freeway.

When the company bulldozers came, the men were kind, but firm.

He took his propane heater. He let them keep his sheet metal roof. They couldn't take his stars.

The Cure

On the same bar stool for two decades, as the clientele got younger, Hank's best setting was dissatisfied. His worst was furious.

Furious hit its peak when Carol called late. She couldn't pick up his prescription, a prescription he wouldn't need if that stupid foreman at that lousy shop hadn't...

Forget it, Hank thought to himself, You've told the story a million times.

He hobbled to the pharmacy, cursing his niece, silently, he thought, when a woman his age opened the door for him.

"Who you cussin 'out?" she asked, and Hank fell in love for the first time ever.

Brushed

The paintings Terrance created were photorealistic, real concept cars, hidden away in vaults near Detroit test tracks, unveiled once a year at auto shows through Terrance's depictions.

Margaux had a science degree she was wasting, bartending at Terrance's favorite haunt. They wound up in bed, wound up engaged, and when they disintegrated as fast as they had ignited, she took the breasts Terrance bought her and took a job far away as a meteorologist at a Bible Belt television station.

Six months later, the station manager refused to believe the nudes he found of her on the internet weren't photos.

Application

Formellos was a small company with a large, terrible reputation.

They were always hiring, but people kept telling Cassandra not to bother, that it was a horror show.

And she was terrified of interviews.

When her electric bill was past due, she printed a resume and steeled her courage.

The parking lot was a minefield of potholes. The door lost a screw when she opened it.

She kept repeating their line, "signing bonus."

The interviewer alternated between curt and friendly, sloppy and professional.

Then he said: "One last question. If you don't mind me asking, how'd you acquire the scar?"

American Vocabulary

"Uncle Ronny, for class we're supposed to ask five adults to give us their definitions of five different words. Will you participate?"

Ron discarded his picked clean rib bone, smiled at his niece, and said, "Sure. What's my word?"

"Your word is *hero.*"

Ron nervously patted the vape in his breast pocket.

"Give me another word, sweet pea."

"I can't, Uncle Ronny. You're the fifth person; it's the last word."

"Well darlin', it's a word without meaning anymore. We've diluted it, which was bad enough, but now society bestows it on those who are the antithesis of the true definition."

Stove

He always let the car run before driving. No matter the temperature. No matter the hurry.

He always lit a cigarette inside the car. Like he got more smoke for his money.

Gas stove, please, she had asked. She liked to cook for him. Even when she didn't like *him* anymore, cooking reminded her of the early days, the love, lust, joy.

Finally, she heard the car pull away. Too fast, squealing tires, like someone would be impressed.

Him, his balled fists, and their painkillers.

She held her hand against the electric burner. The emergency room would give her painkillers

Elevated

I used to worry the cops would think my harmonica was a gun.

I got no cans, no cannons. Just some of my sister's markers and some paper.

Sometimes I look at the city and don't draw shit, just play my harp and think.

Sometimes I draw until it's dark.

Last week the building owner caught me on the fire escape.

His grandfather owned the Golden Fleece.

Now he has a bird's eye picture of the old restaurant in my sister's markers.

He says they're never gonna tear down the water tower, and I'm allowed to draw on his roof.

Cuisine

Lee asked the server if they still served the mussels.

"No," she replied. "We're under new management.

"The pescatarian charade of the previous regime was a cowardly holdover from a colonialist mentality that shan't be tolerated by a caring society, particularly in an industry that has been primarily responsible for a rampant, multi—species genocide.

"Tonight's specials are existential alfalfa broth served in a free trade, biodegradable ladle, and unharvested quinoa stems that must be self-foraged from our exterior hydroponic garden."

Lee smiled.

"May I see a wine list?"

"No," the server said. "We don't serve anyone in suede shoes."

Rainy Slushy NYC   **Andy Krieger**

Extricated

The taxi puddle caught an Armani suit mid-thigh and Mitch laughed. People were always cloaked in something: designer clothes, office diplomas, lies, exaggerations.

He felt like Andy Dufresne, though his resignation e-mail was probably still unread.

New York has been a blast, and he would probably miss some of it.

He didn't know where his Mexico was, and he didn't have a Red, but he had chiseled through the corporate granite and extricated himself from the land of facade and entitlement.

He hopped the puddle, not from fear of getting wet, but because he wanted the challenge of the distance.

                                    Inspired by the work of Andrew Krieger

Somebody

"My brother had a lung made from a pig intestine. Lived to be fifty-seven."

Bryan lifted his beer but didn't pull.

"They don't make lungs from pig intestines."

The bartender walked over.

"Scoop says some wild shit. Play along, nod. He's harmless."

Bryan grunted.

"I don't have to agree to anything I don't believe in."

"You having a rough day? Buy ya a shot. Be nice to Scoop."

"Buy him a shot and tell him to shut up."

"Scoop is a living legend. You're nobody."

"Wait, that's Scoop Parker? My dad loved…

The bartender grabbed Bryan's wrist.

"Too late. Leave."

Thunder and Lightning

Chuck loved to do fat lines of cocaine and chase them with a flaming shot. He called it Thunder and Lightning.

When the band broke up, and it turned into late nights at Linda's loft on the river, it got a little schticky, but it was Chuck. The guy who kept the party going when the crew started dwindling.

One night, he showed it to some newbies after the bar and dropped fucking dead.

Linda choked back sobs outside the funeral home.

Mikey consoled her.

"It was his high wire act, his head in the lion's mouth. He died happy."

Holy

Berwicki felt bad for the guy as he cuffed him.

It was just gonna be a psych eval, but the guy's handwritten books, dozens of them, would be left on the street.

Nolan called in for the ambulance.

"That's a holy book," the man repeated for the seventieth time.

He stared at Berwicki. "Officer, you have to read page forty-three"

When the guy was gone, Berwicki picked up the book.

Nolan called him the next day.

"Wicki, you hungover? You're late.

"That's a holy book, Nolan, really."

"Shutup, man, get to work."

"I quit, Nolan. You gotta read page forty-three."

One Flight

Cowley moved into a cheap apartment, two down, two up. Gloria, directly above Cowley, was heavy, noisy, rude.

Darnell upstairs was a night owl, heavy drinker.

Michelle across the hall was a goddess. Petite, friendly, beautiful smile.

Immediately, he was on a mission to date her. *Shit, I m borderline gonna stalk her*, he thought.

He waited nervously for her to get home from work, wondering if she was in his league.

Before she hit the top step, he asked her out.

She turned crimson.

"I was going to ask you to help me move back up to Gloria's. We reconciled."

A Minor Complication

Jackson was getting more religious as he aged, and his racetrack superstitions were still renting a room and not leaving. It was an odd mix.

Right before they wheeled Deidre in for heart surgery, Jackson promised himself he would never lie to his daughter like he had to her Mom. The divorce had torn Deidre apart.

The day she was discharged, Deidre asked her father what was the best thing he ever spent money on.

They were halfway home when he said, "The blow job I got after Desert Storm. I was just so thankful to still have a dick."

Dirty Money

Kenny was a great kid, but Lori worried about his propensity to lie, especially about his domestic responsibilities.

Lori went to his room, waved him off his gaming headset, handed him a plastic bag.

"Finish cleaning up Shaggy's poop, please, then you can go back to Fortnite."

Kenny said, "This old controller sucks anyway," and headed outside.

Soon he was back inside.

Lori said, "You clean up *all* the poop?"

Kenny nodded.

"Not the poop in the corner by the shed."

"How do you know?" Kenny asked.

"Because I hid ten dollars under Shaggy's pile there for your new controller."

Perennial

She started after Theo died, planting purple flowers in the gaps between the brick at the War Memorial.

Ten years ago, a woman on city council began to recognize Althea for her efforts with a small certificate.

This morning on her walk her flowers, after decades, were gone. Municipal workers were leaving after planting marigolds.

She stood before council the next day, heart racing as the mayor dismissively said, "Chamber of Commerce decided they wanted to go with a yellow theme this year, Ma'am."

Lip quivering, tears cascading, she replied, "If you would've asked, I would have gladly planted marigolds."

Pinball

The timing had to be perfect.

Derek and his production crew got the band loaded into the theater efficiently. British shoegazers, lots of lights, but Derek was done by eleven a.m.

He made his window of opportunity and was at the conference center in time to sign in to the pinball championships.

Free entry, ten thousand-dollar first prize.

Pinball was his first love, before even music.

All the way to the tournament finals, the clock was his enemy.

Letting a ball drain was the toughest thing he ever did, but he won second place, five thousand, and kept his job.

Pistachios

It was the morning after. They showered together, then Barton turned on her TV, wanted to watch some tennis tournament. Ava was trying to be a gracious host. She made mimosas, put out a bowl of pistachios. She couldn't stand tennis. Barton watched tennis. She watched him.

He took the pistachios, shelled them, dropped the shells in a little side bowl.

Held the meat of the nut in his left hand until he had shelled an entire handful. Without eating one. Then he shoved all of them in his mouth at once. She could never trust a guy like that.

Powder

She sat on the grass between the apartment and the alley. Tara had given her the mug her tea was in. Her mascara looked like a Pollack.

Frances, with the Pekinese, came out, invited her inside.

She took powder from a small jar, scooped a tablespoon in Moira's tea.

"You're pale, girl. Come back tomorrow, I'll give you some more."

Moira did. The mystery powder and conversation tradition lasted years after Tara.

Through new relationships, jobs, she always visited.

When Frances was hospitalized, Moira begged for the recipe.

"Powder is simple vitamins. Nothing special. We both just needed a friend."

Rats

On the strip of grass bordering the alley, Norman had three bird feeders and a mat with bowls to feed the feral neighborhood cats.

He watched happily as some starlings dined, flew off, then he grabbed the container of kibble and headed out to replenish the cat bowl.

A sedan pulled into the alley. The code inspector got out, badge affixed to his uniform… mask dangling from his chin.

"Sir, your outdoor feeders attract rats. We mailed a warning," he said, handing Norman a notice to appear. "Rats carry disease."

Norman pointed at the dangling mask.

"So do humans, asshole."

Recital

Neil stopped for a beer.

Leonard, his nextdoor neighbor, called from across the bar.

"Thompson, see you got that Mustang outside the garage. That a '67? If I was you, I wouldn't be reckless with that. That's a beauty. Needs to be cared for."

Neil said, "Using my garage for something else for the next few years, Leonard, thanks."

At dinner, Neil told his daughter, "Sorry we had no room in the house for the grand piano. I took a huge loan for that thing. Do me a favor. Tomorrow morning, play some Wagner. And keep the garage door open."

Art Neely   April 2020

The Art of Living

Sometimes the city streets get empty, and loneliness blows in, silent but heavy.

And then you hear your name, drawn-out and lyrical and enthusiastic. You see a friend, the visual almost unnecessary because the greeting identifies him.

His exuberance cuts through the loneliness like a rototiller through pudding. The joie de vivre encompassing.

"What are you doing?" you ask. The reply, of course, is a concert: the hugest arena act or an unknown singer in a corner bar.

"Why you here so early?" you clarify.

"We're going to the baseball game." An answer you should have known and will remember.

Dedicated to Art Neely April 2020

Nightingale

Trevor sang like a nightingale prima donna from almost birth. On the bus, at the doctor's, in the park.

Adults and children were in awe of Trevor's talent.

Monica felt like the most blessed mother alive.

"Son, one day you're gonna be in a boy band and you will be world-famous."

She took Trevor to some agents.

Trevor wouldn't sing, as though he were a frog in a cartoon.

Back in the park, he sang gleefully.

"Trevor, you must sing for the right people to be in a boy band."

"Momma," Trevor said, "I don't even wanna be a boy."

Snakes and Generosity

The bus was late again. Anastasia looked over to D'Angelo. "What's your favorite animal?" She asked.

D'Angelo didn't hesitate. "The snake. Despite the absence of arms and legs, the snake is capable of propelling itself, and, while not always aggressive, the mere sighting of a snake usually provokes fear, or at least respect. Those who fear it keep their distance. Those who love snakes routinely allow the snake to wrap around their neck. What's yours?"

Anastasia sighed.

"Before you opened your mouth, I was gonna say the seagull because down at Burger Barn everyone shares their fries with the seagulls."

Spark plug

Laura sat in the car, jonesing for a cigarette.

Phil peered into the engine, pretty sure it was a spark plug issue, jonesing for a cigarette.

Laura was convinced he was only helping because he wanted to have sex with her.

Phil pulled the bad spark plug, thinking, *She s never gonna have sex with me.*

He ran up to Cartown and bought her spark plugs and stopped for smokes.

She gave him back way more money than spark plugs and cigarettes cost.

"This is way too much." he said.

"No," Laura said, "in many ways, it's worth every damn penny."

Splashdown

Karl tackled his brother onto the ottoman. Dr. Pepper splashed all over the window.

Parker squirmed away, racing outside, where he fell, needing stitches.

Lillian, nipping her Amaretto clandestinely in the hospital, said the Dr. Pepper had stained the glass in the image of the Virgin Mary.

When they got home, she called a nun.

Karl thought his mom had lost it.

The lawn was packed with people. A man approached their mother. Soon the window was being removed.

It *was* a miracle. The man had paid fifteen thousand dollars for the window, and Lillian used it for alcohol rehab.

Sprinkler

Cam Yaley found a shopping cart with four good wheels and headed for the entrance of the Food-o-rama.

There was some sort of hoopla at the doors.

People in costumes.

Band uniforms. With donation canisters.

Cam spit.

As he approached a voice said, "Support Clarkston High School Band, Mr. Yaley?"

Cam straightened.

"Kyle, when you were a little snotnose you ran through my lawn sprinkler without permission. I told you no, but you did it anyway and broke your ankle. Your daddy sued me. I won, but my homeowners insurance went up and never went back down. Screw your tuba."

Toppled

Larry called his Dad.

"Are you watching? The protesters tore down the statue. I can't believe it!"

Larry's dad said, "Well, that statue wasn't the first. Won't be the last. The artist is long dead…"

"Dad, that's your ancestor! I wrote a paper about him for school. He wasn't a horrible guy!"

"He was a slave owner, Larry. That's horrible enough; trust me."

Larry was on the verge of tears.

"Jefferson owned slaves and he was President of the United States!"

"Well," Larry's dad said, "If we learned anything this year it's that being President isn't reserved for great men."

Tree

He hadn't figured out this social media stuff, but he did like seeing video of the grandkids.

Found out about Laura's death weeks after her service.

He drove to Leamington to say goodbye, though he had almost cried a cataract out saying goodbye dozens of times.

He went to see their tree first. Their initials carved, four years running, starting at fifteen, ending with the draft.

The tree was gone, a lakeside pavilion now with food stalls.

Her headstone was elaborate and stunning. And there, in the middle, was a photo of her, in a sundress, leaning against their tree.

Nine Months

Hughesy was done being sober. He lucked into a free sample of craft stout at the liquor store, pulled forty out of the ATM.

He couldn't go to Casey's or Timeoutz because people there would know him and lecture.

Walked down to Gator's. Place was horrible. Empty on a Tuesday.

Bartender was quiet, heavyset, too much lipstick.

Three beers in she said, "Honey, promise not to steal. I gotta use the ladies 'room bad."

Forty minutes and two self-served beers later, he knocked on the door.

"You okay?"

She grunted, "Call an ambulance. I just gave birth in the toilet."

Whipped Cream

Salamander (crap, did he hate that nickname) didn't hear a sound.

He picked at some ham, sliced for the antipasto.

Later he chose pepperoncini, remembering that capsaicin is a mild pain killer.

He'd been a victim before: high school wrestling, the scapegoat, the loser.

He hadn't seen this one coming. New restaurant, friendly servers.

He hummed when he realized they wouldn't be back tonight.

Even fell asleep for a while, which was dangerous with hypothermia.

He woke when he heard voices, quickly grabbing the whipped cream canisters.

Sucking the nitrous, when they opened the walk-in he cackled in their faces.

Light Up the Sky

The home decor was spare, the drinks were far from stiff, but Steve and Rory thought it was exceptional of their new neighbors to invite them over for dinner.

Rory made conversation with Alice, while Steve carefully flipped through an autograph book full of photos and signatures on the coffee table.

Michael came into the room with some snacks and Steve said, "I feel foolish, but I don't recognize any of these people you're with."

Michael said, "We travel a lot. They are cabbies and concierges, average citizens, and street folks. Whoever treated us well is a celebrity to us."

Cedar Point

The car had gotten hot while they were in the doctor's.

No new tumor growth. Liam wanted to do something to celebrate for Eliza.

Ice cream just didn't seem enough, though it had been a huge treat for him, a foster kid.

Eliza rolled down the window, never complained about the sweltering car.

Liam punched the gas to cool her off. Missed the damn turnaround for home.

"How ya feeling sweetie?"

"Fine, Daddy. It was just an ultrasound. Where are we going?"

"I accidentally missed our turn. And I accidentally remembered neither of us has ever been to Cedar Point."

Chip

Wendy carried in her skateboard, sweaty hair matted to her head.

"Hi, Gramps," she said.

Chuck turned from the TV and smiled at her.

"You're watching golf?" Wendy cringed. "How can you watch golf? So effin boring."

Her grandfather patted a chair. Wendy sat.

"You're into philosophy, right? Perspective? Inner peace?"

"Of course," Wendy said. "All that."

"I can't afford to play every week. I watch these guys. They'll hit a shot from 160 out, leave it on the fringe of the green; they're furious. I think about how damn happy I would have been to hit that same shot."

Melted

After four years in South America documenting the behavior of pythons, Alexandra took a small chunk of her research grant, treating herself to a weekend in San Marino.

She relaxed in the hotel bar, which was sponsoring an ice sculpture contest. Some of Italy's finest chefs were contestants.

One in particular caught her eye as he unpacked his hand tools, examining his ice blocks.

Then he dropped a power box on the floor, plugged in a chainsaw and briefly revved it.

Alexandra flashed back to the decimation of the rain forests, finished her drink, and walked quietly to her room.

Call the Pharmacist

The text from Freddie's aunt said:

Grandpa's pills are in a tray on the counter, marked by day of the week. Give Grandpa his nightly pills, then walk the dog. Understood?

Freddie typed back, *I m not an idiot.*

When he got to his aunt's house, Poochy looked cold chained outside, so Freddie let the chocolate lab into the house with him, watching as the dog bounded through the door, knocked over Grandpa, and jumped toward a roast on the counter, scattering a rainbow of pills everywhere before digging into the hunk of beef.

Freddie texted his aunt: *I m an idiot.*

Toilet Brush

"Saw the picture on your socials. With Jenny..."

Harold's voice had that slow drawl of contempt and accusation that Jeremy couldn't stand.

"...You take her back again?"

Jeremy shook his head and squeezed his beer can tightly enough that it audibly crumpled.

"No, we're not back together, we just … spent some time."

Harold faced Jeremy with a firm hand and an empathetic pout.

"Dude, I see her out at the Rathskeller with other guys. You're her toilet brush. She doesn't think about you at all until things are getting shitty, then she knows you'll always be there for her."

Lord Have Mercy

Nikki passed her phone around as people politely looked at pictures of faded pictures of her singing at the Maryland State Fair.

She looked 1970's beautiful in her gold jumpsuit, breasts spilling out of the deep V-neck.

"Great outfit, Nikki," one of the women said.

"We were supposed to sign with Capitol Records. There was some snafu. We broke up a while later and I gave my life to the Lord. I'm embarrassed by the flesh."

Harold snorted. "The entertainment business spit you out on the ground floor, Jesus caught you and he has no use for the boob job."

Low Pay, But Benefits

Will could have tried to make the bike look newer, but that felt like a lie. Madeline's disappointment was thick and heavy.

All he could afford was a used bike. When he was eleven, he would've been pissed too.

Her eighteenth birthday he'd tell her about his friend pulling the bullet out of his arm, how it wasn't just the bullet, it was the addicts, the damage he caused. Tell her about the four hundred grand left in the ceiling tiles, maybe even his name change.

Tell her how he liked washing dishes because customers could never see his face.

Composing

Nina knew her mother's death was coming, but, as she sat down at the piano, tears washed the keys like a garden hose.

Surprisingly, the melody came easy, even on the wet keys.

She just remembered Momma's favorite songs: the choruses and bridges and tried to blend them like Momma cooking.

But she couldn't sing the words she had written.

She cried so hard she could barely ask Benjamin to sing at the service.

He refused.

She begged.

He refused.

When she walked to the piano at the front of church, he relented.

He sang horribly, but the congregation applauded.

Identity Crisis

Hottest day of the year and Wilcox was purchasing his first brand new car with working AC.

His COVID mask hid a brilliant smile. Wilcox was so happy that when the salesman gave him a cheesy dealership hat to wear, he put the damn thing on.

About a mile from the dealership, there was his adult daughter Amanda, laden with grocery bags, sweating through an already dirty tank top.

Wicox pulled across the street, lowering the window.

"Hey gorgeous, get in!" he said.

Amanda pivoted, dropped two grocery bags, pepper spray hitting Wilcox flush in the eyes above his mask.

Guided Tour

The American streets were lively and exciting to a smal town Irish girl, and Oona was enjoying the vibrance.

"Don't stray too far from me," her cousin Sharon told her. "It's an exciting city, but it's still a city, and people and things aren't always what they appear to be."

Oona was enthralled by the sights and the sounds, while Sharon was bored but wary.

Oona jerked to her right and positively cooed with excitement, pointing at Kruger's Diner.

"That aroma is heavenly," she said, dragging Sharon toward the door.

Sharon pulled back. "That's because botulism doesn't have a smell."

Instructions

Marcy's daily jog took her past the Mounted Police Stables, the kite flying field, the Rouge River.

And recently, past an old woman stretching against a huge, majestic oak.

It took Marcy weeks to realize the woman was only stretching her left side. This morning, she felt compelled to stop.

"Hi!" she said to the woman. "I'm an exercise physiologist and it inspires me that you stretch every morning, but you should really work your right side too."

The woman grimaced. "I'm not stretching. This tree is hundreds of years old. I'm trying to learn her secrets. And I'm left-handed."

Nom de Guerre

The line for autographs was a mile long, ninety-eight percent female, one hundred percent under the age of twenty.

Jonny Z Twelve Thousand signed *Johnny Z Twelve Thousand* on every shirt, record, and live DVD, maintaining eye contact for the first two hours until his neck hurt. After, he took the item, signed, handing it back with a half-smile.

Then an older hand pushed the record forward. He recognized the scars on the hand that taught him to play trumpet and bought his first turntable.

Without looking up, because he would cry, he signed his grandfather's record *Valteri Klimicz III*.

Odd Jobs

Animals were not allowed in the McAllen household. No explanations were given, which was consistent with other decisions. That fact provided logic, but little comfort.

Owen was expected to solicit odd jobs around the neighborhood. He was not allowed to keep the money.

Owen developed a few regular customers, both grateful and begrudging.

Mrs. Sandham agreed to pay five dollars for leaves but always gave him seven.

He would take the extra money and buy a strawberry shortcake ice cream bar.

Owen then sat in the alley, placed the treat on the ground, and waited for the ants, his pets.

Other Than That...

The rawhide bone went from Gerald's toe into the kitchen window.

"Sonuvabitch!" he screamed, and not because the window cracked and spiderwebbed.

Louise's mouth formed, "What the…" but no sound came out.

"The demons at the capitol denied my unemployment again!" Gerald yelled, answering his wife's unspoken question. "There's absolutely no reason!"

Louise picked up the documentation Gerald had slammed on the table.

"I'll call the lawyer," she said.

"Great idea," Gerald said.

Louise took the paperwork and walked into the bedroom to call. She punched one digit before noticing her beloved husband had misspelled their surname on the application.

Release

The effects of Bell's Palsy had gotten him cut off at two bars when he was only mildly buzzed, including one that was actually worth going to, so Blake said, "fuck it" and quit drinking altogether.

The first week he was shaky, but he woke with an erection bordering a priapism a few times, which was good for his psyche.

He missed the chaos of the imbibing life and needed to do something with his time, so he moved his funeral and wedding dove operation into the abandoned, condemned lighthouse and waited, sober, for the authorities to figure it out.

Reunion

Pulling off the interstate she could smell Reilly's Burgers, picture Colin's love poems in his perfect penmanship, see the lights of the soccer stadium.

She hadn't been back in decades.

The last reunion was her 25th-the same year her dad closed the stamping plant, and the atmosphere was ugly, so she declined.

The distinguished alumni award was an honor she could not pass up. She hadn't been a great student but found her path.

There were panhandlers now. She passed them, doling out only sympathetic looks.

A man with a dog held a sign: Anything Helps.

Written in perfect penmanship.

Review

The tiny independent theater had booked some duds before, but Fallon couldn't believe the brutality of the review.

She had to see it for herself, like the aftermath of a car accident.

Like her first and only film, ravaged by an alt-weekly film critic whom she drank with.

The film was terrible. Worse than hers, certainly. She stayed for the credits out of respect.

A lone woman walked up the aisle.

"That was garbage," Fallon said, with a conspiratorial sneer.

The woman grimaced.

"I know. I directed it."

Fallon wanted to say I'm sorry but knew it was too late.

Role Model

From the salon to the hardware store, Deirdre spread her drama.

From her cat's unwanted pregnancy to her father's mystery illness, the entire town of Brookdale got an earful.

Paula admired Deirdre when they were kids, wanted *to be her*. She had been a cheerleader, great at tennis; boys all loved her.

Now she was tanning bed baked, unpleasant, wrinkled, and it seemed the only reason she didn't have any body fat was that her self- manufactured stress burned it all off.

Paula watched Deirdre, dipped her doughnut in her ice cream, and decided she was content to be herself.

One Shot

Blood oozed from Martin's wound, the shooter long gone. Andre, who owned the barbershop, ran up.

"Ambulance is on its way Marty," he said, placing his jacket under Martin's head.

A crowd gathered. Andre shooed them back.

Martin tugged at Andre's collar.

"My wallet..."

"You're lying on it, Marty. I don't wanna move you."

Martin rolled to his left. His breath was labored.

"Please...grab my wallet."

Andre felt like crying. He didn't think his friend was going to live to worry about a wallet.

"Dre...take the condoms out. Please. Janice and I don't use em. She'd be devastated."

Role Play

Even with his glasses, Eric's eyesight was shot. But he had to know.

Standing for a better look, his cane slipped. He grunted as he caught his balance.

Across the coffee shop, two girls rolling twenty-sided dice looked over, then back at their game.

One girl said, "Seventeen. Take entry of the Tunklain portal, not enough for attack."

Eric smiled, quickened his pace, almost late for dialysis, but…

"What are you staring at, you old pervert?" the girl snapped.

Eric looked at their board.

"Looks like I'm staring at someone whose character is gonna die in the game I invented."

Scratching Post

Bryce met Lydia outside a bike shop. After some cajoling, she agreed to a coffee date.

When she told him she was a literature major with a minor in drama, he lit up.

"My cat's names are Macbeth, Puck, Othello and the polydactyl is Caliban."

Lydia liked that, but Bryce could tell she wasn't interested.

Later he met Monica at a wine tasting.

Monica taught orchestra at Performing Arts High School.

"No kidding?" Bryce said, exuberant. "My cat's names are Chopin, Wagner, Liszt, and a deaf one named Beethoven."

"I'm allergic," Monica said.

"I don't really have cats," Bryce blurted.

Soundtracks

The probate cleared up, the money deposited in the appropriate accounts, Millicent bought a condo in what she read was the hippest, most vibrant part of town.

Big city drug use frightened her a bit, but she loved the street performers.

Howard, near the fountain with the twelve-string guitar, was her favorite.

One day she gave him fifty bucks. "I'd rather give you all my damn money than give to these horrible heroin addicts," she told him.

Howard shoved the fifty in the band of his underwear and said, "I'm a heroin addict. I just know how to play guitar."

Don't Let Me Down

The music chatroom Krista Hahn and Bob Street met on was defunct when Krista's urine turned the plus sign blue.

They hugged, giggled, and regretted not having saved screenshots to show their future child the epic arguments over who was better, Krista's beloved Beatles or Bob's obsession, The Rolling Stones.

They decided a few things: the child's name would have no connection to their favorite bands, and that Bob would quit drinking when the child was born.

Krista had a few complications and was sedated after the birth, waking to meet her healthy son, Keith Beast Exile Hahn Main Street.

Swing and Miss

Heinrich proudly pointed to leftfield.

"My grandson," he said.

Dave nodded and pointed to the catcher.

"Evan. His grandfather will never see him play because twelve years ago some useless cocksmooch got in a fender bender with him and went all road rage, sliced him like a Christmas ham and left him to die on the side of the road, alone."

Heinrich was shocked at the raw emotion. "My condolences," he said.

Evan struck out to end the game.

He was still crying when Dave got to him.

"Why are you crying?" Dave said. "You need to get over things."

Traction on the Platform I

Eduard scanned Gwen's family photos, one too many glasses of Cabernet in him.

"How did your mom lose her legs ... if you don't mind me asking?"

"Accident, "Gwen answered graciously. "She was the first person in her family to attend college, got hired at a law firm right out of school. There was a snowstorm her very first day.

"She was late, running to catch a commuter train. She always told me she was terrified she would slip running up the stairs. As it turned out, she made it up safely, then couldn't get any traction on the platform."

Traction on the Platform II

The girls were playing soccer, neighborhood league, idyllic fall afternoon.

Krystal and Gretchen watched their daughters sometimes, but mostly conversed about life.

"The world's rougher on these kids than it was on us," Krystal said. She was about to pry, and she knew it. "I worry about my daughter. You can decline to answer. I wouldn't blame you, but the scars on Felicia's arm look … self-inflicted."

Gretchen nodded. It was painful, but she was happy to discuss it with another mom.

"Bethany wanted so badly to be a Tik-Tok singer. She just couldn't get any traction on the platform."

Verses

Being in the thrift store suit made Vincent uncomfortable, both physically, from the bad fit, and from the ego perspective.

But he had an entirely different persona for his paid liaisons. He wasn't the slick, Christian marketer who made millions off bible verse car air fresheners.

He was Karl, a struggling appliance salesman who liked to be completely humiliated.

The girl entered the car, which was a beater he kept behind the office strictly for these dates.

They went over the details, and "Karl" began to drive.

"I hate these stupid air fresheners," she said.

It was a good start.

Village People

The scar on Carter's lip made him appear to have two lowers, only slightly mitigated by a permanent tobacco stain. Most of his stories included being "up shit's crick" and heroically escaping. His frequent companion in the stories was the woman tattooed on his bicep with the dahlia in her hair, though any good tattoo artist would tell you she's an anonymous flash design from the Korean War era. Hank didn't give Carter money to tell tales in front of his store on the restored cobblestone path in the village, but old Carter was priceless. Hank hoped he'd live forever.

Zoo Train

The zoo train picked up at the flamingoes and dropped off at the elephants. His grandma would bring him to the zoo; they'd ride the train. He stopped coming as a teen because he couldn't stand the cages. He grew up to write songs about freedom and peace. Some of the cages became habitats, some bars on his own personal cages began to close in. So he went back to the zoo, rode the train, like when he was a kid. Kids asked for his autograph now. He asked their names, and signed his, with the inscription, *Never be caged.*

Arrival

Ethan stood in the on-deck circle, scanning the weather-worn bleachers for his dad.

He'd be next to Mr. Densmore, probably, but he was nowhere.

Gunnar walked, bases loaded.

The game was midseason, didn't mean anything to anyone except a handful of kids and their coaches.

Ethan took the count to two and two.

He stepped out of the box, one more look to the stands. No dad.

Next pitch hung, and he drove it deep to right, gone. As the cheering faded, he heard the world's loudest Harley pipes, and his dad, on his Fatboy, saw him cross home plate.

Amplified

The fretboard of her bass was showing through the worn parts of the soft case she'd inherited from her uncle. The pills were turning her eyes a kind of sunburst, at least in the reflection of the chrome fender of the bike the studio loaned her.

A bag of weed would get her through the recording session. Shit, a joint would do.

A skateboard clattered and bounced into her leg, coming to rest against the fountain.

The kid's elbow was bleeding. His apology shot past Betty's ears as she saw her band's logo tattooed on the arm above the blood.

Depth Perception

They came down through the mountains, onto Main Street, still quaintly named Main Street. Alicia proudly pointed out the Indian restaurant, Vindaloo Village.

"We aren't too backwards for a small midwestern town."

"I'll pass on Indian food," Bosman said. "I had a bad experience in Spokane."

Alicia shook her head. It wasn't gonna work.

She had no poker face, and Bosman picked up on it.

"What's the big deal? I don't like Indian food anymore."

Alicia pulled over, looking straight at Bosman.

"It's not the food; it's the concept. I still swim in the lake where my little sister drowned."

Mustard Seed

She was raised in captivity. She did not know her imprisonment and the invasive horrors at the hands of her uncle were abnormal.

When the barn door splintered, she thought the men with the radios and guns were evil, though she didn't know what either implement was.

They got her a home and a woman that talked to her, helped her. At seventeen she learned about the world outside the barn.

The woman took her to a place to eat where the sandwich mustard came in tiny packets. Some mustard was discarded inside them. She wept for the mustard seed.

Flame

It was cigarettes vs. booze, and Janelle was about to crack.

She'd resisted the part of the bet that mandated smokes and vodka must be in the house. George insisted that beating temptation was key.

Five hundred bucks, and, of course, bragging rights to the winner.

Janelle couldn't fight, wouldn't fight it anymore.

Mom's lupus was worse; they bumped her to third shift; she deserved a smoke.

She lit it, inhaled deeply. Hated herself. She let George win. He smiled and grabbed the envelope.

She threw the smoke in his coffee cup and noticed a light blue halo of flame.

Thriving

"Her custom cupcake shop is going under."

"Her trust fund, on the other hand, is thriving."

"Must you always be bitter? She's devastated."

"She can recover on the beach in Belize."

"You could have made something of yourself, despite your hardships."

"You love Wilma Rudolph stories. She's the exception, not the rule. Besides, 'something 'is subjective. Guys would kill to be shift supervisor, have my parking space."

"Your friends would probably kill for less. She's on her way. Please be nice to her."

"I was nice when she said people would pay 22 bucks for cupcakes. I shouldn't have been."

Tether

Sylvia insisted on the tether. She was afraid Thaddeus would get abducted.

Barry clipped his sleeve to his son's sleeve, a retractable cord between them.

At the zoo, he bought Thaddeus caramel corn, because Sylvia thought popcorn and sugar both caused cancer and Barry thought she was full of shit about everything.

Thaddeus loved uniforms. He wanted to talk to the policemen standing by the kangaroo exhibit.

Sylvia hated cops.

Barry unclipped the tether from his son's sleeve, and Thaddeus happily ran to chat with the policemen.

When Barry crossed the Kentucky border, he threw the tether out the window.

Focused

Friedman's mother was organized to a fault.

Too old to send her outgoing mail, she still stacked in alphabetical order.

He dropped it in the mailbox, smiling at the letter asking to be on her favorite game show. She sent it every week, decades after they only took email.

Friedman was shocked when they invited her.

She was a whiz at the game, adored the host.

Friedman sat in the front of the studio. "Ring in, Ma!!"

She was silent.

Conveyer

"You lost the finger in an industrial accident, Mr. Lazar?"

It took Ernie a second to comprehend what his new physician was saying.

Then he looked at his left hand, and up at the doctor, who was around the same age he'd been the day his finger got stamped off and continued down the conveyor with the bus bumper.

"I didn't lose it, Doc. I donated it to my brain to remind it to save up all my money and go to work for myself, so I didn't keep working for a guy who didn't care if I got maimed."

Second Helpings

Cherie returned from her second trip to the buffet line at the office picnic, sliding a slice of peach pie in front of Tommy.

"Laura makes it every year. Superb."

Tommy shook his head, forcing a smile at his new manager.

"I don't eat dessert, thanks."

Cherie blushed.

"I'm sorry, are you diabetic?"

"No, not diabetic, just ...ummmm…"

"Um what?" Cherie asked." I'm curious."

"You know how I'm a caregiver for my sister?" he said.

Cherie nodded.

"Someone at a picnic laced a pineapple in a Jello mold with 75 hits of LSD. That's why I take care of her."

Dedication

She'd always felt like they were meant to be together.

He'd said as much in late-night, presumably (and sometimes admittedly) drunken texts.

They had been too young for it to last, truly, but there was still something there, after all these years.

She could work from anywhere now.

Why not Seattle? Why not near him?

His first book, advance copy, lovingly dedicated to her. His second released today, and she was first in line.

She began to read it in her car. Her birthmark was on page fifteen, and the rest of their sex life followed.

She called her lawyer.

Letter

It was his last bottle. His choice, this time.

There was about a quarter left and maybe one more paragraph to finish telling her everything; the full Tommy gun intensity of his love for her.

Where to find the money.

She could meet him in Windsor.

The blood vomit derailed writing temporarily.

The letter's lines had gone from painstaking perfection to dancing a waltz of their own.

He reread the final paragraph and took a copious swig.

Warmed, he took the stamped envelope and slid it inside the secret lining of his briefcase.

Tomorrow, the whiskey would tempt the coroner.

Biography

His paper route wasn't a job; it was an excuse, an escape, a safe haven, except for Florentine, the customer with loud birds, who always wore a robe.

But even Florentine, who, if he was a predator, never captured his prey, was preferable to running out of scotch rhapsodies and single act shouting matches in the bungalow.

And there, at the end of the route, was The Fortress: his own abandoned building, a dry cleaner once, maybe, and now a dusty cinderblock palace in which to eat chemical formula snack cakes and read comics until he had to go home.

Drowning Caterpillars

Five sheets of paper seemed excessive.

"Zachary, our daughter is six. How is her weekly schedule five pages long?"

Brandon rubbed his husband's shoulders.

"Calm down; look at it. It's totally doable. We're gonna put a ton of miles on the Volvo, but Ashley's worth it."

Brandon read out loud. "Skating. Introduction to Coding. Beginner Lacrosse. Asian Cooking for Kids? You're out of your mind, Zachary. Introduction to 'no effing way'."

"I want our little butterfly to spread her wings and experience the world," Zachary said.

"That's great, honey," Brandon answered. But I don't want our little caterpillar to drown."

Giftwrap

Charlie couldn't stand baseball, but Paisley was the greatest niece, and she wanted a very special, expensive aluminum bat.

Yoga was close enough to the sporting goods store, so Charlie walked over after their session, plunking down way too much money for it. Eschewing an over-sized plastic bag, Charlie took the receipt and rolled the bat up in their yoga mat.

The humidity was ridiculous, so Charlie cut through the Harbortown alley for some shade.

The dumpsters reeked. The shortcut was a bad idea in general. Then Charlie heard a menacing catcall. Paisley was gonna get one slightly used bat.

Old Normal

"What do you miss most about life before the virus?"

Kazper didn't hesitate.

"Tamales."

Adrian squinted. "You can still get tamales, weirdo."

Kazper shook his head.

"Not like I like em."

"What kind of tamales went away?"

"The kind you get down on Fort Street, where you say hi to the lunch shift counter girl with the world's most beautiful smile. You eat one with your bare hands--no sanitizer, no gloves--while walking to the river. Kind you eat while Dion fishes for carp. You throw some masa in the water to attract the carp, but Corona took Dion."

Saturday Chill   John Bunkley

Passionate

My mother inspired passion.

"Whatever you do, you gotta have passion."

She used to say that she'd rather hear a bad singer with their voice filtered through heart than a good one who was content to hit notes.

I own an ice cream truck.

Painted the damn thing myself, with pride.

My passion is painting and making little kids smile. They run down the street, all I gotta do is tap the brakes. They scream with joy.

That's powerful; that's love.

Sometimes I give some ice cream to the poorer kids.

I gotta get passionate about finding a new transmission.

Inspired by the art of John Bunkley

Postmarked

The postmark was still legible. The address was not, smeared by some unknown liquid.

Could have been vodka, morning water, cat piss, tears.

Seven years ago, in a town Cranston had lived in but could barely remember.

The letter carrier fell.

He'd swear to whoever his higher power might be that he meant nothing but good: help the letter carrier.

Heat stroke.

He called an ambulance, grabbed a handful of mail and left.

No clue why he still possessed the envelope.

Proposal

Marty led the way in his kayak. He circled back around to smile at the most beautiful girl in the world.

He and Laura met on a group paddle trip, just fourteen months ago.

She had been so shy, and still was. Embarrassed about her first marriage, naked only with the lights off.

He knew little about her, it seemed, but he knew that he loved her.

The ring was in his bag. He guided her to a small island in the river.

She shrieked.

"Just a bee sting," he said as her whole throat blazed and began to swell.

Puddle

Wilkins hated being late, and he was late. He knew a shortcut, took it, racing.

He cut Ashton so it would basically be a U-turn onto the freeway and punched it.

Needed new wiper blades. Accelerated in further frustration.

The car was roostertailing a huge puddle when he saw the white dress.

He saw the water cover the dress in slow motion.

He skidded to a stop. The white dress hung over breasts worthy of a magazine.

He rushed to apologize, stammering sorries and bits of excuse.

A voice said, "You got a towel, man? My dick is getting cold."

Technically, She Did Say…

The divorce had gotten ugly. Marilyn was so pissed at Peter. Bryan was letting slip about his father's drinking habits and tantrums. There hadn't been any violence, but Peter swore like a sailor, raged, and Marilyn's sweet little boy was starting to emulate him.

Marilyn promised Bryan a pet if he got straight A's. He did.

The adoption fair took place at the zoo. Marilyn had promised "any" pet. The animal rescue offered puppies and kittens and lizards and bunnies.

The families at the zoo that day won't forget Bryan screaming, "You said any pet! I want a fucking hippo!"

Temper

Nedrey was famous for tearing shit off walls. Beer mirrors in bars, phones at the few jobs he kept, a painting at a gallery, when he was dating the artist.

Schwartzy and Coston kept telling him to grow up. He laughed at 'em.

Started dating the hottie from the snackbar at the driving range.

Schwartzy wanted to warn her about Nedrey's temper. He didn't, but Nedrey showed her anyway.

Nedrey was shoving jalapeno poppers in his mouth at Silo's when Schwartzy approached, tears in his eyes.

"She's dead, Nedrey. She didn't know you ripped the wires from the CO detector."

Attention Wars

Kevin took his towel and hangover fighting beer to the pool.

He placed his ample gut on the chaise lounge.

Mari called out, "Your son is very proud of his Lego skills. You should probably give him a little praise for it."

Kevin nodded, hit his beer, closed his eyes.

He woke hours later, sunburned and miserable.

Standing, he heard and saw plastic blocks cascading to the pool deck.

"Kids," he muttered.

Entering the master bathroom, checking himself in the mirror, his shoulders were sunset red, and the middle of his back was the pale outline of the Millennium Falcon.

Atlas, Shrugged

His dog waste removal business folded; he lost seven
hundred bucks on some new crypto out of Guam; he was
getting about two hits a week on his surf ballads.

Eddie called Laura anyway.

"I know we're not together and stuff, but like, when I have
money, would you let me take you to Europe?"

Laura reclined her car seat.

"Hypothetically, Eddie? Sure, I suppose I'd consider that."

Eddie beamed.

"Really? It would be a blast! "Italy, Ireland, Argentina…"

"I'll give you two weeks to come up with the money, Ed.
Please don't buy train tickets from Ireland to Argentina."

Running Late

Larry was second guessing his choice of tie as he tied it but was running late.

Bella came into the master bathroom looking tense.

"The freeway is covered in a human blockade and the police have McNichols closed off too. Might as well call in. If you made it to work, you'd be hours late.

Larry hung his head.

"When are these damn protestors gonna stop? They made their point."

"You can discuss that with your daughter," Bella said.

"Angela's here?" Larry said, puzzled but happy.

"Yes," Bella said. "She came here last night to wash off the tear gas."

Spell It Out

Edie and Marcus ate dinner in the backyard. The conversation was sparse, the chicken overcooked, and Marcus was his typical grumbling self.

"Why," he said rhetorically, "do these freaks make signs in the overpass fence with Styrofoam cups? *Jesus is Lord. Are You Saved?*"

He chewed asparagus and continued. "It's ridiculous. You can't save souls with Styrofoam cups."

"They wanted your attention," Edie said, "and they got it."

Marcus grumbled. "It's still stupid. A waste of time."

The following Friday, Marcus made his way home, and there in the fence above I-94, the sign said, "*Make Love to Me, Marcus.*"

Difference of Opinion

"That rent seems awfully cheap for a view of the river."

Ken sighed. It was audible over the phone.

"You've always been a cynic, Guillermo. They're just nice people, not gougers."

"What do they do for a living that allows them not to be gougers?"

"Political consultants," Ken said. "I don't know which side of the spectrum, don't really care. I gotta do light maintenance, mow the lawn, bring in the mail, which is what I'm doing right now."

"Political consultants?" Guillermo asked, rhetorically. "I never trusted that job."

Ken laughed at his friend's paranoia, then Guillermo heard the explosion.

Knot I

"Oh Jeezus. The comedian is performing a wedding ceremony."

"That's like the least funny thing I can think of."

"Not a lot of people here. Not a lot of friends. That's sad."

"Not as sad as marrying the girl I fucked Wednesday night."

"Wait...what ?"

"Yep. That's her. No question."

"The one you texted me about. With the...the one who did the thing with..."

"Yes, that one. I should tell the guy."

"Why, Billy? They're exchanging vows *now,* not Tuesday night."

"I know, but I assume..."

"Don't assume anything. It's none of your business."

"I feel guilty."

"You shouldn't."

Knot II

"We paid to laugh, not watch someone get married."

"Jen, the cynic, strikes again. It's cute."

"It's different. But they could have warned us."

"Oh shit! I *should* warn her! That's Mike, from the other night!"

"What other night?"

"Mike. I texted you about him."

"Wait, the magic tongue guy?"

"Yep."

"You gotta tell her."

"And ruin the best night of her life? She doesn't even know me; she'll just…"

"Make him tell her. Confront him. I would."

"They are saying their vows tonight, not before. It's none of my business."

"You would want someone to tell you."

"Maybe not."

Knot III

"Who gets married by a comedian?"

"Everybody should, because it's a joke."

"Crap me sideways, Phillip, the groom!"

"He *is* good looking."

"He looks *great* naked. He's hung like…"

"Shutup! The groom is gay? And you've had him? This wedding just got more interesting."

"Monday night. Fantastic. Very oral, very attentive."

"I wonder if she knows?"

"Maybe she's gay too. Maybe it's a big poly party and I just got us invited."

"We'll congratulate them and find out."

"Oh, hell no we won't. What if she doesn't know?"

"She needs to."

"If she doesn't know, she'll find out soon enough."

Linnaeus Be Damned

A child danced into the clearing.

Children were not Gilvey's favorite. He laid down his brush.

"I know the names of all the birds!" the child's voice said.

She pointed at a flock of loons that had not fled her high-pitched voice.

Gilvey knew their names too, having painted them at the Sanctuary for five decades.

The child rattled off nonsense words for the loons. Gilvey smirked.

A woman approached. "I'm sorry if she disturbed you," the woman offered.

A crane took flight.

"A bandalooopernuff!" the child squealed.

Gilvey smiled.

"No disturbance. I believe she just named my next painting."

Invisible Walls

The message on her art Instagram was legit. Andrea found herself three hours from home, painting a mural on the outer wall of a large independent grocer.

It was a seemingly idyllic town, though all towns have tensions, secrets.

On day four, she began to feel like she'd learned the fissures of the place by osmosis.

She walked into the store owner's office, brush in hand.

"Though I'm an independent contractor, I've noticed I'm your only black employee. The streets and Google tell me this town's 24 percent black. I can't paint diverse faces outside, when there are none inside."

Spin the Globe

The oncologist gave the grim timetable. Weeks.

Cynthia really didn't feel that unwell, for such a dire diagnosis.

As they pulled into the driveway, Bernard said, "I'll make reservations for the Grand Hotel. It's your favorite place on Earth."

The word Earth triggered Cynthia.

"No, Bernie, that's sweet," she said, "but I spent forty-two years in the office at the landscaping company, thirty-five in this house and every other vacation at the Grand Hotel. Earth, my darling, is a huge place."

Bernard said, "Anywhere, my precious flower, you name it."

"Across an ocean, Bernie, and don't book a return flight."

Exploration

"I gotta tell ya, at times it felt like I was all alone."

Miriam nodded, as Brant paced around the kitchen, describing his experience.

"Ya know, it's not just the silence; it's the feeling of disconnection and the what ifs.

"What if something happened?

"And I don't just mean to me. I mean, what if someone needed my help?"

Miriam felt like her eyes would roll out of her head and onto the floor.

"For the love of crutches, my intrepid friend," she said,

"You're not exactly Lewis and Clark. You walked five blocks to the store without your phone."

Extended Family

After the ballgame, Evan stopped in the park.

Having skipped school, he couldn't get home this early.

Pigeons milled about, squirrels, moms pushing toddlers.

Evan realized he had half a bag of peanuts left. Couldn't take 'em home.

Cracked one to lure a squirrel over. One crept toward him.

"Don't feed him. That's my squirrel," a man said.

Evan stared.

"Shutup old-timer. Nobody owns a squirrel."

The man glared, opening a small picnic basket.

He unrolled a checkered cloth and brought out a buffet of acorns and caterpillars.

"Lunchtime, Fred."

The squirrel in front of Evan scurried to the man.

Facade

Though she loved her mother, Adrienne hated the woman's all-out worship of money and status.

It seemed incongruous with her religious idol, who ministered to the poor and infirm.

But they had to find peace. Adrienne would be stuck living there while she finished her masters.

Adrienne wandered the self-help section of the bookstore and ran into Bryan, who owned Skull Atrocities, the world's coolest art, record collectible, store.

Her mother always made the sign of the cross when she passed it.

Adrienne chuckled as she phoned her mom.

"I'm going to have a dinner guest. He's a business owner."

Exterminators

Erik thought the mouse was his pet. Too young yet to realize it was multiple creatures, he delighted when it scampered out from crevices.

Hanna thought Erik was squealing and giggling at the small TV, perpetually on.

The neighbor kid brought her smokes and handed her flyers from the porch for pizza and exterminators. He stared at her bottle.

Erik saw two mice at once and squealed until he drooled.

A strange man came into his room. The mice ran.

The man had a picture of himself clipped to his coat.

He took Erik to a place with no mice.

Rare Books

"The Roger Staubach cover of Life Magazine, if you can find one, which you probably can't, is worth a ton of money. They pulled the cover after Kennedy was shot."

Herb sat down, reluctantly.

"You didn't call me here to talk about Life Magazine, Charlie."

"This is called 'softening the blow', Herb."

"Why's there a blow in the first place, Charlie? I have a contract."

"And Cawlins Harpoon Publishing has a loophole, which they exercised."

Charlie ordered two beers with his fingers.

"They scrapped it. Herb. They don't want a novel with a white cop hero, and I don't blame 'em."

Shattered Image

With condolences ringing in his ears and royalties plummeting, Darrell did it. Sold the beachfront place, moving into his late mother's house.

It was a nice house, nothing to be ashamed of, but…

He had lived the rockstar life for so long it seemed backwards, out of character, out of image.

He emailed his team the address: manager, attorneys, publicists.

Then he plopped on a tacky chair next to the hen figurines and the horrible meadow prints.

His publicist texted:

I'll be over shortly with the girls who won the Meet and Greet contest.

Darrell felt like smashing some figurines.

Flying

Like any little boy, he wanted to fly.

There were swings at his special school that looked like rockets, hung from four chains.

Kids would make them buck, like a horse. The chains would scream but hold.

Teachers would reprimand the kids.

He was a good boy, but he wanted to make the rocket buck, like turbulence. Like his life.

He gathered courage late one recess. All the other kids were getting in line.

For the first time he got out of line. He made the rocket buck. It threw him. He flew.

No one saw him, but he flew.

Expiration Date

"Bradley's dead. Yves is in custody."

Sandy sniffled softly.

After a long silence she asked Robby, "You think, in the ambulance, still conscious, Bradley thought Veronica was worth it? Like, if he knew the relationship would cost him his life two years later, would he do it anyway?"

Robby pulled a beer from the fridge.

"People spend billions every year asking services to find them love. When the perfect love the service found them doesn't work out, they spend more money, repeating the process. Bradley and Veronica found each other. He loved her. He'll never lose her. He'd answer 'yes'."

Strange Music

She asked that they meet at her house. He thought it strange, and dangerous for her, but he did not decline.

She gave him a tour.

He marveled at the musical instruments, the stacks of notebooks.

She played him a piece on the viola. Her blue eyes sparkled, blonde hair dancing.

Her skin was the color of a football, and so dry she looked like she could shatter.

She recited poetry over the beautifully arranged notes.

He finally asked, "What beach is your favorite?"

She cringed.

"No beaches. I have a bed. I haven't left the house in eight years."

Family Tries

"You've never had sex with a man?"

Tommy Marlow's dad wasn't a joker, but Tommy asked anyway.

"Are you joking?"

"Your sister told me you were bisexual." Bryan Marlow could not have said it more calmly.

"Miranda told you I was bisexual?"

Tommy's father nodded, again, calmly.

"It didn't seem that farfetched. Warren's gay."

"My best friend being gay doesn't mean I am. Why would Miranda say that?"

Bryan's eyebrows danced.

"Maybe she thought I'd write you out of the will. She'd get it all."

"Dad, I didn't want to tell you this, but Miranda's..."

"Then don't," his father said.

Plastic Wrap

Angie wrapped the casserole in plastic, which, of course, ran out.

Angie was tired of making meals only to refrigerate Terri's portion while she worked late.

It wasn't even late anymore. It was regular.

She wondered what their yearly plastic wrap expenditure was.

Sure, Terri was making great money.

But tonight would be the last meal. Let Terri order delivery when she got home.

Angie decided to spell it out in refrigerator magnets.

"The Last Supper." She was nodding out on the sofa when Terri arrived. The door slammed.

Angie heard the magnets and her reprieve scatter on the floor.

Population

The afterglow was in a bodyshop. Carlos liked cars.

Stories of his life were slurred, sometimes exited with, "You had to be there."

The only glow now was a clip light reflecting off the melting bag of ice that blanketed the last five beers.

Someone said, "The town got smaller."

Someone else said, "It doesn't seem right."

A new glow erupted in Tony's eyes. He grabbed a can of spray paint. They ran to the sign at the edge of town: Welcome to Pinebluff, Population 2743.

A little spray paint, some tears and laughs later, the three became a two.

Preordained

The executive vice-president read her professional accomplishments while a list of things she had done in her thirty years at Fairfax scrolled the screen.

Of course, the speech extolled her perfect attendance. She accepted the rather garish crystal they presented her, gave an exactly five-minute speech and politely received the applause of her peers.

Damon embraced her warmly, though he was just her beard for corporate events.

"Does it ever get old?" he asked, "being perfect?"

"Yes, honestly. It's a lot of pressure. But perfectionism is how I'm wired. My parents must have known something when they named me Constance."

The Hulk

The clothes were strewn about the bed, an absolute mayhem of colors and patterns, nothing remotely matching, but Sylvia had promised herself that her child would make their own decisions for themself as to style and identity. They hadn't gone too far over budget.

As Terry ran outside to play, Sylvia was proud and felt like she was making good parenting decisions.

Hours later Terry ran back inside, dirty, shirtless, brand new purple pants shredded beyond repair

Sylvia blanched and gasped, "Terry, is being destructive part of some new personality you're exploring?"

Terry nodded enthusiastically.

"Yes, Mom. I'm The Hulk."

Things That Have Strayed

Distance and dollars had arranged it so that Callie Reznick was meeting her grandfather for the first time at fourteen.

She had heard stories, but he didn't have internet access. This would be the first time she saw anything but a still photo.

Callie knew how he lost his left index finger, but she asked him anyway, and he matched the story her mom told, covering every detail.

Same with her favorite story about his band.

He had a tattoo on his bicep. *Betsy.* Her mom never told her.

"Who's Betsy?" she asked.

Grandpa grimaced.

"Sadly, I don't remember her."

Wristwatch

Trent dropped his change leaving the store.

Bending, he picked it up. Didn't want the bums to have it.

Near the curb, he saw a wristwatch.

Chintzy band, scuffed faux gold. He left it.

Stopped at Rollo's. Got a scotch.

Larissa's makeup was smudged.

"Lost my grandma's watch today."

"No shit?" he said. "Were you at LiquorLottoDeli?"

"Yeah, got smokes."

Trent jogged back. One of the downtrodden guys was trying to sell it.

"That ain't yours, old man." The man turned away. Trent swung.

After the cops arrested Trent, the bleeding man walked down to Rollo's to sell the watch.

Alien

Hawthorne chose to recline in the stinging nettle. Everyone knew this edge of the lake was full of it. Nobody would disturb him.

He'd been yearning for something since…forever. Since his kindergarten teacher crush, since baseball tryouts…wanting…anything.

A true orphan, now nineteen, not knowing what exactly he wanted.

There was a flash. It wasn't lightning.

Whatever the blue glow was that was burning his eyes felt like it wanted him. The glow opened. Can light open?

The visitor in the light beckoned. Hawthorne was a wanter, not a dreamer, but he was about to travel a dream

Accident Prone

The bar door swung open. Fisk immediately knew it was Leonard. They had been best friends since ninth grade, remained best friends in college even after the potato chip heir had t-boned them drunk, stayed best friends while they were rehabbing their injuries, won the lawsuit, drifted apart.

Leonard had upgraded to a more modern prosthetic.

Fisk had downgraded to cheaper whiskey.

They hugged and Fisk said, "How's Janice?"

"Janice left me. I can't father children."

"Damn chip boy," Fisk said.

"No, not our accident."

Leonard, false teeth and all, smiled his old mischievous smile.

"Hit a dock waterskiing stoned."

Hunger Sun Fruit

The burn scar on Marty's arm looked like a child's fingerpaint drawing of a fruit on a stick figure tree.

Or maybe he was still high.

He was still high.

The sun was behind the clouds, but he knew it would be obnoxious, piercing before he made it to the drainage pipe.

The construction company left the pipe when they finished the freeway.

Just left it to be adopted by the skaters, the taggers, the junkies.

The pipe would be crowded soon, when nightfall hit and people traded stories about scars, shared stems, despair, and a hunger for more dope.

Good Grief

The new house was supposed to bring some peace.

Bianca allowed herself one picture of Terry, on the enclosed porch.

The pumping music from next door made the porch unbearable; by three a.m., she was on the front porch of her new neighbors, banging on the door.

Finally, the door flew open and a very drunk man leaned out.

"Who are you?"

"I just moved in and I recently suffered a death in my family..." Bianca began.

The drunk neighbor grabbed Bianca and hugged her.

"Us too! This is Danielpalooza! Day One," the neighbor said, handing Bianca a champagne bottle.

Fire, Water, Air

If one could sprint through a sunset, shattering it, she would have.

Sunset wasn't the end of a day on a calendar, it was a place of escape, a portal of universal fire.

In reality, she finished her run in waves over her head and gracefully relented, letting the tide carry her back to shore, collapsing where the shallowest rivulets of water teased her feet.

Life is a series of tarnished fantasies and polished sins, pinballing about in an arcade of expectations.

Freedom is relative to the length of the chain and, if you're lucky, you breathe imagination like air.

Man Bun

A man bun?

Melodia had heard Bringo changed, but she wanted to retch when he walked through the doors of The Ornate Horned Frog sporting a man bun, the follicular equivalent of a neon "Douche" sign.

In fairness, she had wanted to retch from the five passionfruit margaritas she'd consumed to calm her nerves for what she hoped would be ravenous nostalgia sex, after Bringo paid her back the two hundred she'd loaned him to buy a black market puffin in college.

Bringo hugged her, she puke gagged, and he gently placed the hairpiece full of cocaine in her hand.

Unbuckled

There was a full tank; that was a bonus.

Hallemeyer never would have bought the damn crossover if he knew Liza was gonna kick him out four days later.

She said, "Get a motel room." He decided to. Seven hundred miles away.

In the mirror he could see the baby seat.

He wasn't coming back. He wasn't gonna play that game.

He stopped on the Jefferson Avenue bridge, shoved the small garbage bag in the baby seat and threw it in the river. He saw a man dive in after it as a woman screamed.

Hallemeyer didn't correct their assumption.

Knock it Off

Parents and kids milled about the alleys, picking up trash as part of a neighborhood beautification project.

Two women reached for the same discarded cheese corn bag, nearly butting heads.

They laughed, and Donna said, "You're Avery's mom, right?"

Patti smiled. "Yes, Avery's mine."

Donna said, "Best dressed kid in the whole school. Designer everything."

Patti blushed. "Designer knock off. I make them myself. Go to the store, take some pictures, buy some fabric. Boom."

Donna smiled. "Wish I could do that."

Patti ventured, "Sewing not your thing, huh?"

Donna replied, "I can sew, but I'm an intellectual property attorney."

Hearts

Gerald's cardiologist begged him to take the stairs, but it was elevators every time until he ran into Henry.

The embrace contained some of the tremors of the memory.

He wondered if Henry suppressed the memory or had organically just forgotten.

Does one forget something like that?

He hoped the girl forgot.

When his own daughter'd been young, he knew that he would've killed men like himself and Henry.

In his mind, Henry, all these years later, grew in fault and in blame.

Gerald took the stairs now, sweating out his own guilt, all the while bragging to his cardiologist.

Clean

Freddie took the job at the car wash because he needed the damn job.

There were three ways you could work at the car wash.

Washing cars, washing cars and selling weed, or drying cars and taking money for the weed.

Freddie played straight the first three months, but minimum wage was a joke.

He just didn't want his mother to know. Too many loose jaws in the neighborhood.

Four months into the job, Freddie's mom pulled in.

"Freddie, they tell me you're selling weed."

"That's a lie, Momma."

"OK, Freddie, can you introduce me to someone here who is?"

Last Wish

Aaron's decline was too precipitous to allow for home hospice. Maryann talked the nurse into bringing their cat Pesky to the hospital.

The kids, all five, made it back, thank heavens, and each got to say a private, personal goodbye.

Maryann went last, breaking her promise to herself, almost immediately, that she wouldn't cry.

Aaron's already weak voice was thin and nearly inaudible from speaking to his children.

His wife bent close.

"I just wish," Aaron rasped, "I could truly convey to that cat how much joy he brought me over the years."

Aaron closed his eyes and slipped away.

Method Acting

Margaret didn't return Rick's calls after the backseat incident. Schnapps was involved and a painful collision between his knee and the metal clasp of a seatbelt. She was polite when they ran into each other weeks later. They never saw each other again.

Margaret remembered it sometimes. There was no fancy term for what happened when they were in college, not publicly anyway.

Rick was on set, thinking about Margaret for the first time in years, prop fishing pole in hand.

Weeks later, Margaret's favorite game show ended, and there was Rick on an infomercial hawking medication for erectile dysfunction.

Keepsake

Arlene had spied the doll in the window the day after Ford had been sworn in as President.

Her mother couldn't pull her away fast enough, denigrating the doll, its foreign origin, the little thrift store, and the state of the world.

Arlene began to make her own money, and walked past the store often, both puzzled and sad that no one had bought the doll, but she wouldn't disobey her mother.

The thrift store was padlocked as Arlene circled the block with her team.

She considered telling her associates the doll story, now that she owned the whole block.

Traffic

Craddock told Johnny that Cindy was nanny for Orlando's kid now, started at noon, after the kid's preschool.

He had tequila for breakfast instead of beer, worked up the guts to throw himself in front of her car.

Ya couldn't miss that yellow Fiero.

Damn car was too small to kill him, but he'd get her attention, let her know she ruined his life.

He got to the corner early. He saw the Fiero, took a step toward the curb.

A LeSabre turned right in front of him.

"Johnny!" Booker yelled through the window. "Welcome back. Let's grab a taco."

Wipe Your Mouth

Edwin was tired of juggling his inventory liquidation business and the mayoral duties of Branchgrove.

Tonight's duty was entertaining the pastor of some Redemption...something church: a huge one under construction.

Edwin set the table. The pastor arrived, unexpectedly saying yes to a glass of wine.

Edwin graciously poured the good stuff and grabbed two beverage napkins.

Giving the pastor his wine, he retreated to the kitchen to get some snacks. When he returned, the pastor held up the napkin. It read "Happy Marriage Daniel and Nicholas."

"This offends me," the pastor said.

Edwin smirked. "You prefer a straight napkin?"

Opera

He laughed that she got all the opera questions right on Jeopardy.

He slurped his beer and told Larry, "Every opera question. A fucking bus driver. She knows all the opera."

She hated how her husband spoke about her.

She wasn't just a bus driver, dammit.

She was the mother of his twin sons.

She was working on a Master's.

The week it clicked, the week it became real, she waited patiently.

Then, as the theme music played, she muted the television.

"I'm divorcing you, Bob. You don't appreciate me. You've never once offered to take me to the opera."

Alarming

Antoine swore that a falling leaf could set off Marsh's car alarm. It always seemed to be right after Antoine's head hit the pillow after a rough nursing shift.

He left notes, sent emails. Marsh made unkept promises. This morning's cacophony was unbearable.

After forty-five minutes, Antoine walked outside, groggy. Could he pop the hood, disconnect the battery?

The damn car was unlocked. So much for security.

There was a half eaten powdered donut on the front seat. Antoine opened the door, grabbed it, pushed it into the gas tank. It was mean, but Antoine wouldn't lose sleep over it.

Heat Sensor

The Chapmans inherited rural property from Ronald's Uncle Bob. Melissa was thrilled, until Bob's passion for hunting flooded her husband.

Almost overnight he was buying gear. They'd been vegans in college.

She protested his new hobby to no avail.

He sat, watching his heat sensor camera from his computer, looking at deer he'd soon slaughter.

The rift in the marriage widened. They spent more time apart than together. She asked for a divorce. Ronald slapped her.

Melissa left.

Weeks later, Ronald sat at his computer. On screen, his wife leaned against a tree naked, another man's face between her legs.

Dating

He asked all the questions he thought were the right questions.

Some were important to him, like what her favorite books were.

He liked two on her list, though they weren't favorites.

Other questions just fit the "normal" mode but were of little consequence.

Eye color was a risky one, especially because he didn't care.

"You can't tell from the photo?" she asked. "They're brown."

"And honestly," she said, "I 'shopped the photo slightly. I'm heavier than I look."

He sighed.

"I didn't look at the picture."

"Bullshit!" she screamed, but there was mirth in it.

"I didn't. I'm blind."

Clarity

His brother's face came into focus.

Harry said, "Hospital's gonna transfer you to alcohol rehab."

Sean groaned. "I wasn't driving, why am I here?"

"No recall?" Harry asked.

Sean shook his head.

"You weren't in a car, but you were kinda driving. According to the cops, you and Wilson walked to the zoo. Broke in. You were riding a capybara. And you missed Gwendolyn's powerlifting meet."

Sean sneered. "Her meet isn't until Saturday."

"It's Sunday morning," Harry said.

"I did not drink enough to lose a day, Harry."

"The zookeeper," Harry said, "had to shoot you with a tranquilizer gun."

Impotent

She opened the door. In sweats and a loose t-shirt, she makes his head warp with desire. Maybe it has gone beyond sight and is a frontal assault of pheromones by an unrelenting horde.

She puts on jewelry he can't commit to memory. Just her is enough.

"You're insane," she says with a smile, but there is truth and trepidation.

Later she will be naked, the most beautiful sight in his long life.

His penis will fail him. He knows there are crueler things, but he would trade for them, ravenously.

Take a limb, he thinks. Any appendage but that.

Caterer

Nick didn't have to answer, but he knew the guilt would eat away at him.

"Hello, Mom."

"Can you come over and change a lightbulb?"

He looked at the car clock. If he got lucky, he could make the trip in 90 minutes and be back for pool league in time.

"On the way."

"You sound exasperated," she said.

"It's not convenient, Mom, is all."

As a kid, he had been a ring bearer for four weddings, all of them hers. Two in such quick succession, he fit in the same suit. He wished the last one had stuck around.

Fatalities

He leaned against the fence at the hill above the freeway, either exhausted or intent.

The traffic from northwest merged, heading north, and from southwest merged, headed downtown. After the seventh day, Ellie had to know.

"Excuse me," she called from an escapable distance. "You've been out here for a week, standing here, alone. Everything okay?"

The man turned and smiled.

"I'm just fine. No luck yet, but I've got two more weeks vacation."

"Luck at what?" Ellie asked.

"Internet says this is the deadliest freeway interchange in America. I've seen a few crackups. No fatalities yet, but I'm confident."

Condolences

Devin, somehow, was a healer. People always said she made them feel better.

More than just a good listener, more than just someone with the correct words for the moment. She had no psychology degree, nor any aspirations, though right now she hoped her special skill was in full bloom.

The courtroom was emptying. The mother of Devin's father's youngest victim was standing with her attorney.

"Mrs. Henson, I'm Devin Hornaday. Arthur Hornaday's daughter. Your poise and grace throughout this horrible ordeal are beyond…

The bereft woman squinted, repeating, "Hornaday?" before nudging her attorney aside and spitting in Devin's face.

Medication

Frank served that bowling guy his tequila and checked his phone again. Nothing from Autumn.

He guessed that was good, but surgery for Liza might not be the worst.

He noticed his hand shaking as he refilled the anchovy olives.

Sam from the softball team was giggling uncontrollably. He had just gotten there, still sweaty.

Frank poured 4 beers.

Sam was still giggling.

He asked Stacy what Sam was on.

"Some new designer stuff Billy has."

Frank's phone hummed. Surgery for Liza. He could tell Autumn was freaking.

"Hey Billy!" Frank called. Billy came over. Frank bought two for later.

Neighborly

On nice days, Stan's Liquor's parking lot was an asphalt garden party. Cops didn't seem to care.

Living next door to Stan's was Dusty's favorite thing in the world.

Guys from all the tool shops would cash their checks and drink. They'd be in coveralls.

He lived next door. He could change.

He couldn't change for Gemma. She left him, no surprise, but then Stan went under.

The building was vacant two months. Eyesore. Dusty got drunk, took his tools, removed the big illuminated "Stan's" sign. Hung it on his garage. Invited the boys over, but it wasn't the same.

Slackline

The girl was on a slackline, performing difficult pirouettes and rolls, seemingly oblivious to the giant hulking ore hauler.

No one was near her in the small riverside park.

Richard absorbed her solitude, honored her concentration.

The island east of the city was packed with bathing revelers, the passing speedboats always prone to drunken flashers, but they had become like stripes that create the argyle.

The slackline girl did not perform for the ship or expose for the amusement of the lonely sailor.

He was not particularly lonely, but the slackline girl shared something with him he would always cherish.

Trash

Four p.m. The sun was the kinda hot that would melt the popsicle and immolate the stick.

Oscar and Max had walked five miles to get to the Shores for trash day. Rich people discarded tons of valuable stuff.

Oscar ambled over and rested on a toddler's swing in the park.

Max was exhausted but thought hanging on kids 'swings was the type of thing to make cops start asking questions.

They clearly didn't reside in the neighborhood.

"Great idea to trash pick today," Max said.

Oscar blinked. "I'm too smart to be sane and too dumb to be rich."

All His Shots

Lucas finished the last of his malt liquor and pulled what remained of his unemployment check out of his pocket.

Sixty-three dollars.

Greasy asked "What ya thinking about doing?"

Lucas counted the money again and said "Gonna go to the zoo."

Greasy shook his head. "Zoo's cool, man, but it's expensive; you'll regret it."

Lucas shook his head at Greasy more aggressively.

"No, man, they're having a pet adoption today. Gonna chat up some of the volunteers."

"Makes no sense, you can't have a dog," Greasy said.

Lucas shrugged. "But I know for a fact the women there like strays."

Homesickness

The bunk creaked when he rolled over. He couldn't sleep on the top bunk. He was too shy to ask to switch.

Barry, the kid on the bottom said, "Are you masturbating, kid?"

Nicky said, "What's mathburating?"

Barry said, "Jerking off".

Nicky said, "Jerking off what?"

Barry and a few others started laughing.

Nicky said, "I'm not jerking anything off, I just can't sleep."

"Homesickness," another kid said.

"I'm not homesick," Nicky said. "I hate home."

"Why do you hate home, kid?" Barry asked.

Another voice said, "I'd hate home too if no one there ever taught me to masturbate."

Umbrellas

It was the anniversary of their first date.

"Cannot believe you remembered," Yvette told Dana, dead serious.

Dana pouted slightly, disappointed in Yvette's lack of faith in her.

"Get in the car," she said.

Yvette hopped in. Soon they were at the Riverview Creek Shoppes.

"Pick out anything," Dana said.

Yvette cringed.

"You did this for my birthday and Christmas. It's sweet, but I'd love a surprise gift."

"I got my mom a vase when I was a kid. Envisioned beautiful bouquets in it. She used it for umbrella storage at the garage door. You pick your own gifts, forever."

Alzheimers

He brewed the tea, putting an ice cube in it because she wouldn't have the patience and she'd burn herself.

As he turned toward the living room, she cried, "Oh Lord!"

He rushed in, relieved that she was on the sofa.

"Is this our state?" she asked, panicky.

He hesitated, looking at the tornado dancing across the television screen.

"No, no, it's not in our state."

The tornado turned a truck stop to shrapnel.

She began to cry.

He returned to retrieve the tea, promising himself that tomorrow he'd select puppies on the Animal Planet instead of a movie channel.

Aura

The line to park at the convention went for a mile. Miguel had his hundred dollar pre-order autograph ticket, but now he'd be at the back of a huge line to get a signature from his idol, arguably the greatest sci-fi actor ever. It wasn't about the scrawled name; it was about being in the man's presence.

Miguel took his place in line and smelled booze. He turned behind him to see a man in an Iron Man mask, unsteady.

Iron Man giggled. "Been at the hotel bar all morning. Always wanted to see this nonsense from the fan's perspective."

The Pen, The Sword

Summer camp, they both agreed, had been some of the highlights of their lives.

Putnam, the spy novelist now, world famous. Evans was still in Saginaw, running a plumbing business.

Putnam met Evans for lunch at the taco joint that was once the breakfast place on their paper route.

Evans pushed the book in front of Putnam. "Sign it to 'The Best Plumber in Michigan'."

Putnam stared at his old friend, quietly disheartened, took the silver pen, signed.

In his truck after lunch, Evans opened the book and read, "I don't do endorsements, Billy Evans. You still wet the bed?"

Free Radical

The frosted glass on the bathroom window once was a source of comfort as Erin dashed around getting ready for work.

The tenants of 12B across the way had always been guys, and more than once she had felt eyes, caught glances.

Then she got to know Bradley, who hung out the 12B window to smoke.

He was hanging now.

She lifted the frosted glass.

"Hey."

"Hey," Bradley said, "How was ummm...ya know...surgery?"

"It sucked," Erin said. "It was supposed to suck." She pulled her towel aside, flashing Bradley the mastectomy scars. "But I'm recovering. Thanks for asking."

And on Your Left

Sid sat in the city bus shelter for a little free shade.

He heard the guide from the rental bus tour describe the brutal massacre which happened in the house on St. Aubin, near the market. The woman knew her stuff.

Not ten minutes later, a bike tour halted, the guide offering an entertaining, vivid account of the events that had transpired in the house. Sid knew the account was largely fictionalized.

Then a walking tour. The city had gentrified to the point the tourists weren't afraid to walk.

They strolled past the house as though nothing had ever happened.

Antihero

He had watched the World Series in that family room.

He had mowed that lawn while they were away.

He had climbed on the roof of that house and lowered gifts down the chimney with fishing line to give his best friend's kids a Christmas thrill.

The chimney had collapsed on the family room, firefighters were on the lawn, and Sarah kept tugging at him saying, "There was nothing you could have done."

His right foot itched, the one that would have started the run, but he had frozen in fear and had never come closer than smoke and regret.

Wine

Marcella's friends warned her he drank too much. She glanced at the wine bottle in the ice bucket, smoothed her dress, and checked the time on her phone.

He was seven minutes late.

He couldn't possibly get too drunk on half a bottle of wine, and she considered drinking more than her share.

He was a brilliant attorney — the best-looking man in all of Bay City. If he drank that much he'd be bloated and gross, right?

She was tempted to start drinking without him.

She heard brakes screeching and her mailbox flew through her dining room window.

Bears & Wolves

The Tacoma rains had accelerated her love of interior activities, and Uncle Nick's gift of a microscope took Alexis from lonely, dour child to Queen of the Tardigrades.

She imagined riding the tiny beasts into battle against her enemies, real and perceived.

She wasn't interested in the science, just the fantasy, until her friend Betsy read her tarot cards, telling her she was destined for greatness in the world.

Betsy was the only person in the audience who wasn't a PhD as Alexis, water bears dancing in her head, accepted her award for clinical research in the fight against lupus.

Harmonica

She wondered if other people in the motel complained about his harmonica.

Every time she kicked him out, he walked down the street playing.

She would cool off, go get him a few days later. Always the same motel, always the harmonica.

Dylan, The Replacements, stuff she didn't recognize.

He always came back, and she always told him she would work on her temper, her attitude, her meds.

She drove to the motel. No Jerry. No harmonica.

Three more motels. Nothing.

The tent cost eight bucks at a garage sale. The birds on Belle Isle seemed to dig the harmonica.

Death and Texas   Aimee Chorkey

Witness

"It's just a tragic masquerade, Charlie."

Morris knew Charlie wouldn't tell him who pulled the trigger, just wanted him to understand.

"All these jerkoffs talk about their shiny guns like they're vintage cars. The Russian and German words roll off their tongues like they found a new wife in Volgograd or Cologne."

Morris could see blood splatters on Charlie's socks, his valet uniform pants just a bit too short. He was close when it happened.

"You don't have to tell the cops, Charlie. You don't have to tell me. But tell someone, because, if you don't, you'll lose your mind."

Inspired by the art of Aimee Chorkey

Straightforward

Maybe it was because her dad accidentally stepped on her foot when he asked the question. Something triggered her. Or maybe Charlotte wasn't giving herself enough credit for simply being ready.

Either way, the conversation went like this:

"Honey, why is there a box of inflated balloons and streamers and stuff in the garage?"

Charlotte stood, hugged her father, and called, "Mom!"

Her mother walked in the sliding door and Charlotte said, "I was going to leave you a dramatic and colorful presentation to let you know I'm gay. Like, attracted to girls, gay. But that would have been cheap."

Handyman

"Hey! Can you give me a hand with my truck?"

Christoff looked at his older brother with contempt.

"I hate when you say 'give me a hand'. You're lousy with engines, and you want me to help you fix it for free. So you should say that out loud when that's what you want."

"'Give me a hand 'is just an expression," Olin said.

Christoff nodded.

"I understand that. You know the feral cat I domesticated? Every night he curls up in bed with me, falls asleep on my right hand. It's relaxing, symbiotic. Giving you a hand is neither."

Inventor

"Remember Alston?"

"The comic book loser?"

"Well... he was kinda…"

"Kind of a dumb turd who doodled men in tight pants on his notebooks? What about him?"

"Just won an award from the State of Michigan."

"What did he do, animate their stupid tourism ads? I hate those…"

"Invented an app."

"So you can draw some alien with a magic ring on your phone?"

"Something to do with blood pressure monitoring. They say it's saving lives."

"No way that pudgy bastard did that by himself! Gimmie a break! That guy was a nothing!"

"How many pills you take a day?"

In Loving Memory

Dakota was almost gone at thirty-two, barely grasping Kaylee's wrist. One last request.

Don't make me promise to quit smoking, Kaylee thought.

Dakota rasped "Please, please, keep the promises you wrote down on our fifteenth birthday."

Kaylee blubbered, simultaneously laughing and crying.

It had been six months, the promises magneted on her refrigerator with a ticket to the show.

Her favorite band from her teen years. Two original members, including Roger.

Kaylee went, got backstage. Met Roger. He was wrinkled, heavyset.

"This is weird," she said, "But I promised myself and my dying best friend I'd have sex with you."

Metamorphosis

First day on the window replacement job. John happily climbed the ladder to work on the upper floors of the rundown house.

His new boss, Burke, was a gruff sort, but he wanted to impress.

Nice to know someone was rehabbing a house in this forgotten neighborhood.

Through the old windows he could see trash, bottles, needles.

And a leg. Decomposing.

"Burke, there's a dead body up here!"

Burke barked, "Landlord's got a guy that cleans up inside. We replace windows."

John swallowed. "Burke, it's a human body!"

"It was," Burke said, "Now it's junk. And junk ain't our job."

Blown Glass

Ilona had been told she was beautiful her whole life. She was cognizant that it must be true, though her career in ophthalmology is what brought her happiness.

She ate lunch at the strip mall near the clinic and watched a glassblower.

She wanted to learn, but no time.

So she was content to watch. It became an every lunch event.

The artist sculpted a sitting woman with large breasts. Months later, Ilona realized it was her, eating her lunch, breasts utterly disproportionate.

Her hair was wrong too.

She introduced herself, handed her card, saying, "I think I can help."

Blood in the Sink

Dalton shaved with his father's old straight razor and brush, antiques both. His father handed him down the alcoholism gene too, more than likely.

He was proud that the bullets were scattered in the grass, though he would have to find all six before he mowed.

Distracted, he cut himself, feeling nothing but seeing the triangular sheet of blood in the sink.

Can you make a vow in a mirror?

Dalton did. He vowed he would never end his own existence, sell his gun to his brother, and purposely cut himself shaving every day for the rest of his life.

Samaritan

Eddie woke to the sound of a drill. Through his own mental fog, he realized he was still drunk.

Three days until his piss test. He'd have to straighten up.

Drill stopped; there was cussing.

Old man next door was installing a novelty mailbox, a World War Two fighter plane.

Eddie went for smokes. Old man's mailbox was on the ground. The old post he'd drilled into was rotted through. Wind had grabbed the wings of the plane.

He bent to pick it up, snatching a few pieces of scattered mail.

A voice said, "Tampering with mail is a felony."

Destinations

Every August, after their anniversary, Malik flew to Vegas. Laura flew to Florida.

Malik's dart team competed in an annual tournament. Laura went to Clearwater to visit her sister.

For five years of this seventeen year tradition, Laura had been entertaining her nephew's orthodontist in a solid week of expensive Malbec and athletic sex.

Malik played a lot of darts, hit a strip club or two and mostly missed his wife. For the first time, they would bring home first place.

Malik brought the trophy to the airport.

Laura decided it was the year to tell Malik to brace himself.

Challenged

Reggie was the first one at the family reunion, and before Ronnie could open the screen door, Reggie said, "Hey Big Ron, how's the police academy treatin 'you?"

Ronnie shook his head.

"I quit, Uncle Reg. Just wasn't for me."

"Wasn't for you? Kid, you never played cops and robbers when you were younger, you just played cops. It was your dream. You shouldn't let anything derail you from your dream."

"My dream changed."

"Nonsense," Reggie said.

"Remember how Braden wanted to be an astronaut?"

"Sure do," Reggie answered."Do you remember he stopped wanting that when the shuttle exploded?"

Fugitive

Security footage airing on the Channel Three news clearly shows Ryan, his first cousin.

But I'm not calling no hotline and turning in my cousin. Certainly not for bank robbery.

He knew about the smack issue but didn't think his cousin had gotten that desperate.

Five minutes later Ryan's wife pulled into the driveway.

Without a wave or a word, she went to the trunk of her car, pulled out a suitcase.

Marching toward Carson, smiling, she said, "I'm staying here for a few weeks. They caught him. He and I are done. I brought PlayStation, and I brought condoms."

Exhaled

A disheveled kid, maybe twenty, was sitting on the stone. The plaque dedicated to the firefighter the park was named for was on that stone.

Disrespectful.

Raymond could lecture, but what good would it do?

"Scuse me," the disrespectful kid said.

"No money, no cigarettes," Raymond said.

The kid said, "I don't want a cigarette. Moved here three months ago. Job didn't work out. Just learned my Dad died in Tucson. I...I can't go back. I just need a hug."

Raymond rolled his eyes. Pulled a menthol from his pack.

"Here kid. A cigarette is a hug from the inside."

Inspired by Jackson Krieger

Chaos and Children's Books

Buck did a lot of Adderall and worked on his children's book, *The Plaintive Plantain,* which Zimmy was supposed to illustrate.

Zimmy thought the concept was horrendous for a kid's book, so he did deep bong rips and procrastinated, occasionally throwing Buck an uninspired pencil sketch.
Buck's dad showed up drunk one night, asking Buck and Zimmy to adopt him a grandson.

He was convinced they were a couple because they were both gay.

They were barely friends, much less lovers: just roommates. He left a check for ten thousand to convince them to adopt.

Zimmy's sketches improved. Buck OD'd.

Vehicles

I'm too damn fat for this little 50cc scooter.

Sheree could hear the kids in the park giggling and commenting as she took off her helmet.

Wait until they see what's next.

She walked over to the Summertime Outdoor Exercise group, joining the other women.

The kids, as she predicted, found endless mirth in her obesity as she struggled through the physical motions.

Back on the scooter, she realized how comical she looked, laughing at herself.

The kids often waited for the woman they called the Scooter Slob.

Labor Day weekend they watched her pedal up, smiling, on a bicycle.

Aroma Revenge

The landlord stood, scowling. At midnight, the Sheriff's deputies could legally enter and start placing the Kiernan's belongings on the curb.

Lincoln put the last of his three bags of stuff in the back of his cousin's truck.
The whole block was shifting. Lofts where Section Eights had been.

German sports cars where hoopties once languished.

Lincoln Kiernan had one last project before he left his childhood home.

He reached into the freezer and pulled out a carp he had snagged north of the Fort Street bridge.

Reaching up into the attic, he placed the carp deep under the insulation.

Music Lessons

At first the songs were annoying, abrasive, barely songs at all.

But as the years wore on, and Henry painted miles of chalk lines on the sports fields, the kids taught him to rap.

The first time he rapped he was redder than their football helmets, but the kids laughed with him and their laughter was like a drug.

After a few years, the freshmen expected him to rap for them. He learned the words to some of the kid's own songs and sang them quietly as he sat in a chair getting his old Confederate flag tattoo covered up.

Post-Mortem Photography

Papa said I'm the oldest now; my prayers worked. Bobby's didn't. I'm God's chosen, but I still can't play on the rocking horse. The man's gonna paint eyes on Bobby and they're gonna put him on the rocking horse. Mama says Bobby is with the Lord. Ain't God and the Lord the same thing? I can't cure fever; I didn't cause no fever. I just wanna go on the rocking horse. Bobby can't feel the rocking horse, I don't think. Sheriff shot Mr. Phillips. He was dead. He didn't cry out. I got real eyes. It should be my horse.

Reminder

"No, it was fun. Cedar Point, skydiving…"

"Then what?"

"Not the sex… that was…really; I was…satisfied. That's not even a good enough…it was great, bordering on wonderful…"

"Then why…"

"You don't have pets. And that's…it's important to me."

"You never asked me why."

"You're right. Ok. Why?"

"Before I was born my father was convicted of setting a dog on fire."

Her hand raised to her mouth so fast her ring clicked against her teeth.

"My mother lied. Said I was allergic. I'm not."

"You could…"

"I couldn't. A dog would remind me of my father."

Impressionable

"Jeeezus Christ on a flaming bagel, Andrew, you're fifteen years old. You ain't gonna impress a girl you like by getting her name tattooed on you. You know what would impress her? Getting a job."

Andrew took his mom's advice, applied for and got a dishwashing job at Bon Giorno's, daydreamed about Angela.

Cashed his check. Got a tattoo in Fuzzy Nick's Basement.

Couldn't wait to show Angela.

Found her at Game Stop.

"What is it?" she said.

"A GTO. The car I'm gonna get."

Angela frowned. "Cars are horrible for the environment. My name would have been kinda cute."

How Fast

The stress was unbearable. Her law firm was changing partners faster than her twin seventeen-year-old daughters; she had an ulcer and no desire to be a grandma.

Late to the deposition. Her stomach was burning up.

Maureen saw the flasher, heard the siren, and knew it was her, easily thirty over.

Pulling over, she reached into the glove box quickly, yanking out the paperwork, thrusting it out the window as the officer approached the car.

She and the cop simultaneously noticed the lace panties dangling from her grip, and at least one twin was grounded from the car for life.

Hopping Mad

Paradoxically, the voice had originally come from her own anger.

Now the voice belonged to a toy so beloved it became a TV series. She had become wealthy while retaining most of her anonymity and privacy.

It was wonderful, but Janie Dobson's life wasn't perfect. The current manifestation of imperfection was the mess that was her parent's wedding anniversary cake.

She needed the baker to fix it. The more sternly she demanded, the more fiercely he pushed back.

Don t lose your temper, Janie warned herself.

Finally, she screamed, "Dadblastit!"

The baker laughed and said, "Holy crap, you're Dudley the Frog!"

Table Nine

Just before the bar closed, they began to trickle in, then, after two
a.m., it was like a cattle drive where the cattle were loud and
sloppy—college kid drunk.

Table Nine was him.

Was it him?

She pivoted away, then changed her mind.

She had to see the ring.

"I'll grab Table Nine."

She strode through the dance sweat, the cinnamon whiskey breath
and the drunken shouting.

He barely looked up. But there, on his drunken hand: the ring.
Some regatta championship.

"Call the cops," she said to Denise.

"Already?"

"The guy at Table Nine is him."

Tracked

Born without arms, John ran cross country because he was encouraged.

Some would think *of course he did,* but running isn't easy without the aid to balance of pumping arms.

He got wild applause for seventeenth place finishes. In his mind only the medal stand would suffice.

Television news crews documented what he felt deeply was his own mediocrity.

He had acceptance of his situation, both external and internal.

In school, John was admired.

Admiration wasn't what he thirsted for.

He wanted to ask the media to leave him alone, but that would sound bitter, and bitter he was not.

Unveiling

The council member and the businessman nibbled from the buffet set up under a tent.

The jail repurposing party was in full swing. The citizen artwork on the outer walls had been unveiled, cultural icons where once had been razor wire.

"Imagine," the businessman said, admiring a portrait of Tupac, "years ago, a black kid could be arrested spray painting in this neighborhood. Now, one got a grant to paint here. Progress."

The council member smiled. "Were you here during the painting?"

"No," the businessman answered.

"Tupac sold 75 million records," said the council member. "You don't know the ethnicity of that artist. Progress."

Vegan

Kids were speeding down Junction, as usual, a cacophony of squealing tires.

Damn Mazda turned the corner and destroyed a pigeon. Duane yelled, but the kid was half a mile away No use continuing.

He walked in the house, checked the fridge, starving.

There was a rotisserie chicken. He pulled it out, started peeling off meat like he used to count bills at the casino.

Thought about that damn speeding car. Thought about that poor pigeon. Looked down at the chicken. Took it to the dog.

That was his last meat. Duane didn't want to eat like a speeding car.

Just There

"What was his motive? There's absolutely none."

"We have his work emails. They're like watching that mechanical yodeler scoot up the hill on the Price is Right, just waiting for it to fall off."

"I'll repeat myself. He had no motive to kill her."

The two detectives squared off.

"What was his motivation to go to work? Nothing except money. He hated everything about the job, about his life. He was gonna kill someone. Himself, his boss, his wife. He killed his wife."

"She didn't seem to do anything wrong. She was just there."

The veteran grimaced. "You're so *new*."

Greetings

Hunter's mom vetoed the idea of Hunter's dad's gravestone being the Mack Truck bulldog he'd requested.

Hunter was sad but relieved his dad died not knowing his son was gay. Suspecting, maybe. He was at peace with that.

In charge of the greeting cards at the family's little truck stop gift shop, he began to write his own greeting cards specifically for his tribe.

His mother forbade them in the store, so Hunter sold them online.

They were such a hit, his mother capitulated. She was glad she did.

Upon her passing, Hunter promised himself, Dad would get his bulldog.

Weeds

The cracks in the cement were big enough to break a person's ankle and the weeds in spots could better be described as bushes.

This had been the factory floor.

The rich man who moved the factory out of the country has a plaque a few blocks away.

The words on the plaque are shiny.

The lives of the people who worked here, in most cases, are not.

They survive, like the weeds that were once smothered by an axle factory floor.

They are as, if not more, resilient.

They are treated with about the same respect: weeds and workers.

Childishness

Donna forked an olive. "I'm starting to interview nannies."

Phylicia smiled. "Audrey loved Monique; I have her number. Super educational, reliable."

Donna shook her head.

"Nope, no way. She's like an Instagram model. I'm not having her wandering around half-naked poolside. Little European trollop, no way. She'd be all over Brian in a week."

Phylicia slid her chair back, loudly.

"If she was like that, she would have been all over Nate, and she wasn't, trust me."

"But Nate's no Brian," Donna said. "No offense."

Phylicia stood. "Point taken, girlfriend. Good luck. And you don't have a pool. No offense."

Battering Ram

The argument was over a stuffed animal. A very expensive one, but a stuffed animal, nonetheless.

I would have loved to have been in a position to buy my daughter a $4000 goat.

Or as my ex corrected me at ungodly decibels, "A designer plush ram."

"She's sick," was the first explanation.

And I was spending, gladly, a ton to get her the best care.

"It's her zodiac sign," was the second.

"She's too young to understand that," I countered.

The ex answered her phone.

"Hi sweetheart. Of course, he got you the ram. He's on his way with it."

Kerosene

Rita wiped sweat from her son's brow, careful not to touch his bandaged, burned arm.

"It's a miracle your Aunt Margaret showed up when she did."

Alan nodded. He felt funny. The doctor told him the medicine to make the pain go away would do that.

"Where's Daddy?"

Rita had not chosen an answer but spoke.

"He'll come see you soon."

She didn't know what else to say.

"He's not burned, right?"

She smiled weakly.

"No, he's not burned."

"Mommy, what's Care O Seen?"

Rita flinched.

"Kerosene?"

"Yesterday, Daddy told Uncle Tommy Care O Seen would fix the whole thing."

Firebomb

Rombo's life was divided into before they firebombed his dad's store, and after.

Who "they" was had been a matter of rumor for decades.

Rombo would have loved revenge. His dad was too sick now.

His dad squeezed his thumb and forefinger together. Rombo dutifully lit a cigarette and placed it in the tracheotomy hole.

Mr. Rombowski's bible and his AA coin were on the nightstand.

Rombo's dad touched his rosary, Rombo handed him the bible.

He flipped the pages.

Bomb, he croaked.

His finger was pressed hard against the gospel of Luke.

Rombo stared.

"Uncle Luke bombed the store?"

Join 'em

The trucking company that cost him his leg settled. Hugh went in search of property.

Found a peaceful, rolling tract near a river, amazingly affordable.

Had a home he designed built, watched it go up.

It was after the big machinery left that he began to hear the hums and whines.

They were audible at all hours.

Across the river, through the tree line, Hugh discovered an industrial space, newly built, running three shifts.

It was nearby, but across the county line, different zoning, no recourse.

After sleepless weeks, he decided he might as well ask them for an application.

Historical Figure

The photo section was in the middle of the autobiography, as usual. There were her Polaroids of him, taken on the beach during their insane courtship.

Years later he had hit records, an acting career, while Liza had escaped his addictions and abusiveness into suburbia: a high school principal's career.

She looked at the pages of photos twice, purchasing the book as a keepsake.

Three weeks later her assistant principal took her aside.

Who to blame? Herself? Did the photo editor know? She was mildly upset, but her nineteen-year-old naked breasts looked fantastic in the reflection of the car window.

Elevation

She took her own path.

Nothing resembling a trail, just a way she could navigate the pines, the mountain.

Liberation, knowing that she wouldn't see weekend hikers.

The path she chose wound and danced and caressed her until she saw asphalt.

Goddammit.

Civilization.

From the song of the birds to the rev of an engine.

Why had they even paved up here?

Why a car now?

She saw movement.

A turtle. The road curved.

The engine roared.

She knew why she had come.

The driver would never forget the woman somersaulting into the ditch with a turtle in her hand.

Horoscope

Becky read him his horoscope, Pisces, every morning. Wendell nodded, smiled, and ignored it or forgot it.

He ate cereal and jotted down his sports bets for the day.

Becky would be on her way to her hygienist's job when he made the call to O'Leary.

He belched orange juice as Becky was saying something about a new arrival to the family. They were too old, too broke.

He watched the highlights alone. Westbrook didn't play because his wife had a baby.

Wendell was out two thousand.

The next morning, he massaged Becky's shoulders and hung on her every word.

Getaway

On the good days, it was marital tradition. On rough days, it was habit. Lately, it had been strictly habit. Christopher and Sally sat at the breakfast table on their laptops, discussing topics of interest.

"Guy shot up a hardware store north of the university. Two dead, five wounded."

Christopher crammed some toast in his mouth.

"I'm reading that too," Sally said. "Financial woes. He snapped."

Christopher swallowed. "I've felt like snapping before. I just go to the cottage."

Sally pulled a sausage from Christopher's plate and pointed.

"Well, Mr. Compassion, I'm guessing, with financial woes, there was no cottage."

Itinerary Change

His dad was gentle but thickly serious.

"Your grandfather built this company. Go, but you'll never be hired back. Not while I live."

Austin nodded, knowing his odds were slender. The band would be traveling for years, might never make it. But they would be *on the road*. Adventure. Sexcapades. Gas station burritos.

Two weeks in, Lincoln, Nebraska, nightclub catches fire. No serious injuries.

Nicky saw a light.

"It was the holy spirit, man. I'm done. I'm giving my life to the Lord."

Austin froze.

Nicky continued. "You can have my van. But you can't play my heathen songs

Key Ring

He had a bottle opener on his key ring long after he had quit the bottle.

On the same key ring, the key to the apartment where Deborah had died.

The pharmaceuticals were helping, in the same way a seven-year-old helps push a car stuck in snowbank.

The weed helped ease things, but it was no cure.

He went back to the old apartment.

The building was vacant.

The key didn't work in the lock.

He called the cops and confessed.

He purchased a forty ouncer.

It was twist off.

He waited for the cops.

No need for an opener.

Detroit Love Story

Adults were milling about, getting the streets, trees, and light poles decorated for the American bicentennial parade.

Mick was supposed to help but wasn't motivated. Bartlett pulled up in his Chevelle and hopped out, smiling like the Tigers had just won the World Series.

"Guess who has a date with Jessica Bianco?"

Mick hid his shock. Calmly, he said, "She's out of your league, both in beauty and in economic status. But congratulations, you can borrow my Maverick."

Bartlett laughed. "Why would I take your Maverick instead of my Chevelle?"

"Because," Mick said, "her dad is a vice-president at Ford's."

Snowstorm

Ellie vomited off the second step into the snow. Judging by the sky, the chunky grayish orange puddle would be covered in an hour.

Some hunks of Andouille would be there at the thaw, along with the dog shit, and Nicky's broken toy helicopter.

Ellie took a strong pull of Nyquil.

If that bottle of wine from Lex's work was still in the cupboard, she'd be asleep before Lex got home. She had a full pack of breath mints next to Lex's note.

What did Lex want?

Nicky and I will be living with my mother. Attached is the lawyer's....

Downpour

Will cradled the soggy shred.

He had been as honest with Lucas as he had ever been with a man to whom he was attracted.

Except for the Suboxone detox. That was an omission.

The attraction was mutual, and Will knew it even before Lucas pulled out his business card.

"Call me," had been a demand. When their hands touched, Lucas said, "Soon", and it made Will's toes sweat.

Or maybe that was the detox.

He walked two miles to the Megabus in the downpour, proud of his honesty.

The soak had gone through his fingers. Lucas's card was destroyed.

Ghost Sperm Emoji

Lissa fanned the few sparks in herself to write Andrea one last love letter.

"It," whatever "it" had been, hadn't worked on many levels.

The age difference, Andrea's lack of income, etc. But dammit, the sex, the cooking and the intangibles, the passion, had been great.

So Lissa reached deep and wrote a love note, sending it electronically.

Waiting for a response was too heart-wrenching, so she went for a run.

When she got back, the response to her words was two straight lines of some kind of ghost sperm emoji. She didn't know what it meant, but she did.

For Sale by Owner

The Bowers had to sell their house quickly. Nancy listed it by owner. They started showing immediately.

No time to present it or tweak it.

"This is gonna suck," she told Mike.

"Relax. It will be fine."

The first couple through the door was pleasant enough, seemed to understand.

The man checked the pantry. "Oh, the kid's heights in pencil on the wall! Sweet! Michael Jr, huh?"

Mike swallowed. "Ummm...yeah."

The visitor continued. "Bethany: three feet, four inches, two years ago. How tall is she now?"

Mike said, "Three feet, four. I assume. Unless she grew in the casket."

Evidence

The first thing Martha noticed, when she entered the home to conduct the evaluation, was a grotesque brown stain on a plate.

It was not the type of thing she needed to jot down. She would memorize it and would write it later.

She wondered if the subject made the children eat from dirty plates.

The house was neither neat nor particularly slovenly.

The estranged father was cordial but seemed distracted. Martha noted this, as he darted between rooms, finally returning with a teacup, setting it on the small plate, making her question if she was right for this position.

Napping

Howard exited the car quickly, slamming the door with his left hand.

He wasn't furious, just annoyed, until his shoulder pulled back awkwardly, and his double espresso flew from his hand.

His overcoat was caught in the door he'd just slammed.

It was sleeting at a sharp angle and he was not going back to the coffee shop. He extricated himself and checked the mail.

Markham's proposal hadn't arrived, just a useless alumni letter and his bank statement.

No espresso meant nap.

He crashed on the couch, one hand on the floor.

The repo man stepped on Howard's fallen cup.

What You Wish For

Satcherfield Falls was a beautiful place on the way to another place.

Trudy brought Rebecca to the bridge overlooking the falls, figuring they'd be back on the road as soon as Rebecca began to fuss. Diagnosed early as nonverbal autistic, Rebecca's care altered Trudy's dreams of investigative journalism, and now the surprisingly soothing effect of the falls on Rebecca made the postcard town their home.

Trudy took over the little town newspaper, reporting on weddings and marching band fundraisers, quietly wishing for something, anything meatier, until the day she opened a package and a bloody knife fell to her desk.

Batter

Everything was made from scratch. She would never use store-bought batter mix.

So inside the box of batter mix is where he stored the bullets. The just-in-case bullets.

Whatever that meant.

He knew she was leaving. Her grandma's cast iron skillet gone from the hook and the lengthy note confirmed it.

He didn't read it thoroughly. He didn't read anything thoroughly.

She signed it, "Love," which increased the bitterness.

He made his decision.

He took the gun and the box of batter mix behind the garage.

The box held some fishing sinkers and a note that said, "I'm not stupid."

All's Fair

"Henry," Dot called, "we're leaving for the adoption fair."

"Whatever you do don't come home with a Great Dane."

"Don't worry, Henry, no purebreds. I'm coming home with the oldest dog available."

Henry glued a cowl on his Fockewulf-190 model.
"A lap dog, right, like a Havanese?"

"An old lap dog, a mutt. It's an adoption fair, not a breeder's convention."

"Good," Henry answered, pulling his champagne flute from his workbench.

He poured, hoping his Liberator model would be delivered. He knelt back to work on the Fockewulf.

Two hours later their new Cane Corso mix barreled through the door.

Thumbs Up

Marlon knew it was a bad bender when he woke. IVs in both arms. One hand bandaged like a club. Someone gripping the other hand.

Jojo. Her smile, if it was a smile, was far from sympathetic.

He wasn't restrained, so he hadn't been arrested…

"Want the good news?" Jojo asked.

"Sure."

"I called the attorney. Roy, the one who advertises during hockey games."

Marlon already wished Jojo had started at the beginning.

"Since the fight happened on our property, we might be able to sue the other guy. They're giving the guy's Rottweiler laxatives, hoping he'll pass your thumb."

Daredevil

"I did a horrible thing at that reception last night," Clarissa admitted as she lifted Brendan from bed into his wheelchair with the aid of his hoist.

Brendan lovingly admired his successful leg model girlfriend.

"You were pretty drunk," Brendan said.

"I told that guy from Adventure Magazine that I was going to traverse the Devil's River Rapids with you in the kayak. He said he'd get corporate sponsors. We'd clear two hundred thousand dollars, easily. You can veto it though, darling."

Brendan smiled

"Hell no! Let's do it! I'd rather die on your feat than live off your knees."

Dalyrimple

The foreman, following company tradition, passed out checks on Friday. "Mackenzie!" Mackenzie grabbed his check.

"Dalyrimple!"

Dalyrimple barked, "I told you, I hate my name, call me Mike!"

The foreman shrugged. "There are three Mikes in the shop, Dalyrimple. Gotta use last names."

Bokemczik called out, "Hey Dalyrimple, if you hate your name so much, why don't you legally change it?"

Dalyrimple sneered. "Changing your name is some Hollywood crap. Hollywood is full of faggots."

Behind the grinder someone yelled, "Hey Dalyrimple, this shop has a few gay men in it. If you don't say faggot, we won't say Dalyrimple."

Winners and Losers

"Hello?"

Liza just about screamed when she heard the voice. She'd never gotten through.

"Am I the ninth caller?"

"Um, you sure are!"

"Holy crap! I win the tickets?"

"Of course you do," the voice said.

"Oh my God; what do I have to do now?"

"Give me your name, address, phone number. Come down to the station with your identification tomorrow afternoon."

Liza complied, her voice shaking from excitement.

"Ok, anything else?" she asked.

"All set," the voice said.

Bryan hung up.

He looked at Lucy. "That's gotta be the cruelest thing I've ever done to a wrong number."

Accelerator

Losing his driver's license for a year was brutal. But one phone call to his favorite cousin, Shawn, and at least Chuck had a ride to work.

The first day, first ride, Chuck said, "You're a life saver."

Shawn shook him off. 'It ain't a hassle."

Now, eight months later, Chuck was tired of Shawn driving like he was in NASCAR and drunk.

"You're gonna get us killed."

Shawn shrugged. "I don't really care if I die."

Chuck laughed awkwardly. "Don't you care if I die?"

Shawn answered, "If I don't care about myself, why would I care about you?"

Finish Line

Elizabeth was training for Boston, when she saw Gabrielle struggling with the flat tire. No average flat tire either, belt wrapped around the axle because she had driven too far.

Screwing her training, Elizabeth helped, and it blossomed into something more. Neither of 'em planned it.

She kept planning on telling Abby there was someone else...but, well, you know.

Her training runs got shorter, though there was no lack of calorie burn.

Gabrielle knew she couldn't go to Boston. She tracked Elizabeth online.

Elizabeth posted a personal worst. If Abby hadn't figured it out, that might be a hint.

Fishin'

Mack and Grandpa sat at the pond at the back of the property, two bass already in the live well.

Mack's grandpa was fidgety today, which was as strange as a frog carrying a newspaper. He was always calm.

Grandpa handed Mack a fifty.

"Run to McKenzie's and get me a hacksaw."

"Grandpa, you got five hacksaws hangin'…"

"I want a new one. Git."

Mack got the hacksaw. He was worried about Grandpa. Most people in town didn't like Grandpa. Mack was never sure why.

When he came over the hill, he saw the Sheriff's helicopter hovering over the pond.

Window Treatment

The first thing Grant bought was curtains because the windows of the next apartment in the crotch of the old deco building were three feet away.

As he unboxed the curtains, he saw a white cat staring at him and an Alexander Calder exhibit poster on the wall.

He looked closer and realized that he was doing what he was trying to avoid being done to him: snooping.

He caught a glimpse of a shirtless Adonis in the kitchen, sipping a beer. He folded the curtains neatly, placed the box on the ottoman, and went to buy a Calder poster.

Waffle House

Her town was dust mite small, so it was a thrill to get hired at the Waffle House by the freeway.

It wasn't county peach queen big, but big.

Her aunt's friend had worked up to regional manager.

Then a rock tour bus arrived. Wasn't the first time, but it was the first time after her eighteenth birthday.

This time she said yes.

Thirty-four seemed ancient. Alice's grandma was thirty-seven.

He was nice, but he cried like a baby when she wouldn't take the ring.

She accepted a plane ticket and hoped Waffle House would give her her job back.

Ceiling Fan

The ceiling fan blades were not the "Forest Majesty" she ordered.

All he cared about was that they spun, moved air.

Back in the box it went, after an angry e-mail .

He poured her some wine, and she rubbed his neck, almost reflexively, but tenderly.

Even after a decade, he lived for it.

They were naked within minutes.

They rolled and writhed, then, outside, a terrible crash.

Screams and sounds of panic. He began to speak. She shushed him

"Let's save us," she said.

The next morning, they installed the ceiling fan, together, and forgot what color it was.

I'll Show Them

Admittedly, he was a little bit stoned during his job interview at Grocery Giant, but he had decent grades, promised to be punctual. He was livid when he found out Grocery Giant hired someone else as a bagboy.

So Mark Pollard made it a point to shop at Grocery Giant, once a week, and "accidentally" knock a glass jar off the shelf.

He kept a tally of items he broke: Pickles, baby food, olive oil. Unbreakable plastic was making it more of a challenge, and at age sixty-two, still bitter, he quietly retired his protest having spent thousands shopping there.

Jigsaw

He was too young to know the definition of the term acquiesce, but every Friday night Dylan acquiesced to something.

He knew the word *consequences*; his father had instilled it. Dylan was smart enough to avoid the threatened consequences, but he felt a powerful and growing reluctance to continue.

Lew turned the cardboard box upside down and the puzzle pieces fell onto the card table.
"Do you know why you will start this puzzle without the edge pieces?" Lew asked.

"Honestly, Dad?

Lew nodded.

"Two weeks ago, when you taught me this lesson, you flushed the edges down the toilet."

Maze

She wore the wrong shoes, and she knew it.

Tonight was supposed to be a haunted house, then Rick had decided on a haunted maze.

Outside. Muddy.

The owners threw down mulch, but it was woefully inadequate. Her new shoes were caked in mud.

It reminded her of life. She made the wrong decisions, then tried to cover for herself. Her life was walking on inadequate mulch.

In the cold. With someone who was just a buffer against loneliness...

"Rick, let's separate and see who can finish the maze first."

She dashed off before he answered. Proud of her decision.

Traveling

Their relationship wasn't measured in time; they measured it in miles they had put on Danny's Subaru, visiting graves of the famous and obscure.

Beatriz funded the trips they had first discussed in a chat group before they met in person.

Some of the deceased were musicians they loved, some were unknown by name but their inventions were ubiquitous. Some were infamous for crimes.

Danny was doing a birthdate rubbing when Beatriz suddenly vomited.

The rubbing lay on the nightstand back at the motel. Beatriz gasped.

If she carried what she thought she did, the birthdays were a plausible match.

Intro to Writing

He stared. Julie knew he was staring at her. It wasn't a leer, but it was uncomfortable.

He wasn't at her desk, but in the foyer of the public library, disheveled, worn.

Finally, he spoke.

"You taught the writing workshop five years ago in Continuing Ed."

She couldn't manage a smile but nodded.

"Sure did."

"I wrote a novel."

Now she smiled. "I'd love to read it."

He giggled and ran out the door.

Moments later he returned with a stack of shoeboxes.

"I wrote it on 3x5 cards. They're numbered. Read it. I'll be back Wednesday for your review."

Curfew

When the curfew hit, Reilly knew the Lieutenant would make him and Reeves clear Grifter's Corner.

There were no tourists, no streetwalkers, no dope slingers.

Just the street performers, with no crowds.

The jugglers were juggling. The human statue stayed still, his tip hat barren.

The singers sang, even after Reeves handcuffed one.

Amoeba, the best street magician Reilly had ever seen, just stared, flipping his trick cards in the air, cackling.

Reilly loved his tricks, but not tonight.

"Gotta go, Amoeba."

"Ain't goin 'nowhere, Reilly. You don't have a pair of cuffs that can hold me."

Reilly believed him.

Dandelions

She knocked on the open door of the landscaping shed.

"Help you?" said a pleasant voice.

Tamara said, "Can you not spray herbicides behind 113? I'm harvesting the dandelions."

Marty stood.

"We have to spray every unit, Ma'am. It's our job." Annoyed.

"I'm actually trying to give you less work," Tamara said, "I have plans for those dandelions."

Marty grimaced. "You'll give me no work if I get fired for not spraying every unit. There are more weeds than just dandelions."

"Did you know you can make wine from dandelions?" She asked.

"Not yours," he said. "They're full of chemicals."

Crowned

Conner hadn't been a hat guy until Julie. She bought him one on their first trip. He wore it, a Derby, because that's what you do when someone buys you a gift. Then a ballcap from Cooperstown, a Panama down south. He began to collect them but rarely wore them.

It became his thing, his schtick. He had hundreds on display.

When Julie left, she said the first one was because his hairline was ugly. That hairline hadn't lasted, now nonexistent from chemo. He pointed to the wall and told the hospice nurse to help himself to any of them.

Cellar

Garfield needed a drink. Edging the lawn was his least favorite thing on earth.

The fridge was empty. He was gonna strangle Mortimer.

He stumbled to the basement, angry, parched. He better have his private stash hidden behind the books in the fruit cellar. What if Mortimer found that too?

"If my beer's gone, you're fucking dead Mortimer."

He got to the cellar. The door was ripped from the hinges. Garfield bellowed, "Jesus Mortimer, you're destroying my house! You're a dead man!"

He looked down. Mortimer's head was there. An axe had cleaved it. Mortimer really was a dead man.

Cold

A rare cold snap made DisneyWorld a ghost town. The realtor had a good year, and dammit she was going to enjoy the trip regardless of icicles hanging from closed rides.

Space Mountain! The line was non-existent.

She put on her headphones. PetShopBoys greatest hits. Pure bliss. An amusement ride, her band, upside down at 40 miles an hour. The music stopped. Her headphones were gone. A hand was on her throat. She screamed. She couldn't breathe. The ride stopped. She jumped off, never seeing her assailant. She bled to death at her hotel. A puncture wound she never felt.

Cracking

Old man Kizmara scanned his lottery ticket, Barlow watching closely.
It was a five hundred dollar winner.

Barlow thought about robbing the old drunk, but Barlow, half-drunk himself, remembered how bad he wanted Kizmara's niece, who worked in the garden department of the hardware store
he had to go into every day for work.

If he got busted robbing the guy, he could never flirt with Cheryl again.

He couldn't ask the old guy for a loan; that would be weak.
He was stronger than that.

He went outside, sucked on an empty stem, looking for someone else to rob.

Craftsman

The guitar on the stand was still a beauty, the headstock hardware with a showroom gleam, even though Nick had played it every day for the thirty years after he built it by hand.

The pool cue he had modeled after the four hundred dollar catalog version was in a case, but the trophies it earned were shining back at the metal hardware of the guitar.

He had been capable of creating everything he had needed to make himself happy, his whole life, until now.

The third luster to complete the triangle was the metal sides of his hospice bed.

Cooked

Gabe sold his salmon sandwiches in the corner of the farmer's market, most of his customers: other vendors and friends.

His cousin owned the fish farm and cut him a deal. The sauce he drizzled over the filet was something he concocted drunk in college.

When the pretty girls who took copious selfies became regulars, it livened the little place up.

They said they'd make him famous, and he laughed until, one Saturday, there was a line curling around the block.

He looked over his shoulder at impatient faces and folded arms. Within weeks, his hobby had become a chore.

Collateral Damage

The host of the podcast said, "How did you get started playing the drums?"

It was a simple question.

But it was a minefield.

His mother believed in total honesty. Andre believed in loyalty, even to a man who probably didn't deserve it.

He paused, then chose honesty.

"I always wanted a drum kit. My mother refused. Andre silently said a little prayer, then said the words in public for the first time in his life.

"My father sold drugs. One of his customers owed him money. The only thing of a value the man had was a drum kit…"

Bus

Just five of them on the platform for the bus to Toledo.

An old Hasidic couple, a tall black guy he didn't trust, Marko, and a gorgeous brunette Marko kept glancing at.

It was freezing, but her wool coat was open. She had confidence. He smiled at her.

She smiled back.

"You work at the transmission shop?"

Marko beamed.

"Sure do."

"I work across the street."

"The uniform shop?"

"Next door to the uniform shop."

"That's the precinct."

She nodded.

Marko got twice as cold. His head pivoted crazily.

"Don't move, Marko" she said.

The tall black guy handcuffed him.

Diurnal

She stepped into the bathroom faster than ever before.

Freakishly diurnal, she had awakened with the sun and planned to get in bed as soon as it set.

The smell should have woken her. Can a smell wake? Smoke can, but smoke is tangible.

He was hanging from the light fixture, not the curtain rod, which would have snapped.

He had installed the clawfoot tub, and his bodily fluids now drained into it.

What would 4 extra pills hurt? she had thought. She wanted deep sleep. She had gotten days, her last days to ask him what was the matter.

The Shed

Mark stared at the shed. He'd rather burn it down than clean it out.

Constance showed up while he was procrastinating, she reeked of spiced rum and freshly bleached hair. She had fried it, brittle as pasta in a box.

He could take his knife, cut off a hunk and use it to start the fire that would burn down his misery.

But he promised Nana. So he turned and sprayed WD-40 on the lock, hoping the rust would disappear.

Constance belched and wobbled. The bastard couldn't find the bucket of fetuses.
She pulled Mark's knife and began to stab.

Haunted Attraction

The server set the thick slice of cheesecake down, saying,

"Happy Anniversary, you two."

He paused and said, "How'd you guys meet?"

Paul looked at Nancy with "permission" eyes.

She decided to beat him to it.

"We had sex in a corn maze," she said.

The server smiled widely but bit his lip.

"I'm sorry, I asked, "How'd you meet?"

Nancy nodded.

"We were at the same corn maze on a rainy night; place was deserted. Both got lost; wound up in the same corner. Started talking. I said, "I've always wanted to have sex in one of these things."

Not Registered

Foot tapping at the windowsill, reclining in a chair not meant to recline, Rory's habit of watching way too soon for the pizza guy would never subside.

So it was that he watched a guy with a clipboard shovel a sandwich in his mouth.

The guy then approached Rory's door.

Political canvasser. Rory had done it once; he'd be polite. But the guy had a clump of moist partially chewed white bread on his lower lip.

The guy began his pitch, Rory staring at the errant dough shaking loose from the man's exuberant mouth, hitting Rory right in the eye.

Progress

Delta wanted to nominate her therapist for an award.

In two years, she'd gone from anxiety-ridden recluse to taking dance lessons, having a great social life.

Tonight was the big test: speaking in public.

A political town hall, a candidate she loathed and had been aching to ask a question of.

She was terrified, almost to the point of fleeing, but proud she had improved this much.

As she walked in the slow line to the podium, she steeled herself. It felt like a graduation.

She was next when the moderator said, "That's all the time we have, thank you."

You Never Know Who

It was that Lyman groomed his beard. No, it was his laugh.

It was more than Daniel Villion wanted to admit.

Soup kitchen volunteering seemed natural. He was privileged, bored, and empathetic.

Falling for a man who came to get a meal three times a week did not seem natural.

He was certain Lyman was gay; that wasn't the issue.

The issue was: How does a soup kitchen volunteer ask out a patron?

Holy Angels, that laugh. Those dimples.

Daniel could change Lyman's whole life.

Did Lyman want his life changed?

Would they both die lonely?

Daniel said softly, "Lyman…"

Skyhook

Elkin had, he told everyone, the best job in the world.

He flew his beloved Cessna above sporting events, trailing banners for automobiles and beers.

Then came 9/11. Airspace at large events was severely restricted.

Jennifer Elkin gave birth to twins, and the financial landscape was as restricted as the skies.

Elkin got by, but it was rough. Then the virus hit. There were no large events, no fans, no banners, no money.

So it was that he climbed into the cockpit of his plane to fly a banner for a political candidate he'd rather punch square in the face.

Buoyed

The wedding was opulent, expensive: Olympia's ideas, her father's checkbook.

Now four months later, Olympia had to tell the man who spent six figures on the nuptials that the volatile relationship was over.

Scarlet faced, embarrassed, she explained the situation.

When she finished, her father told her, "My childhood dream was to be a lifeguard at the country club and get rewarded for saving a rich man's child from drowning. I got the job. Never saved one person, because all the kids were good swimmers.

"Forget the money. Your ability to swim without needing rescue is beyond any price tag."

Frozen Memory

"Papa won't eat, Shirelle. I've been cooking him his favorite salmon dish. Nothing."

"Dammit, Lindsay. I'm on tour; what can I do?

Lindsay rolled her eyes.

"He's our father. I wanted you to know."

Shirelle held up a "wait a second" finger to her drummer.

"Call The Caucus Club. Get him the steak we used to get him for his birthday. I'll pay."

Lindsay complied.

The steak went untouched.

The next morning Lindsay helped Papa out of bed.

He stared at her and whispered, "No more salmon. No birthday steak. I want that frozen meatloaf your Mama used to heat."

Wet Socks

Callen purposely walked straight into the ankle-deep puddle.

Laura asked why he did it. Callen shrugged it off with the charming smile: the bullshit, fake, charming smile.

He hadn't been able to go in the basement since he found Veronica's bracelet.

And no basement trips meant no laundry.

The depression was eroding him. His whole life stank.

He was down to his last pair of clean socks.

But they weren't clean anymore. Inside his ratty old Adidas were now wet socks.

He had to brave the basement. He had to grab the detergent and try to get back to living.

Chicken

He was such a xenophobe—a word he hadn't heard—he wouldn't call it Russian Roulette. He called it "gun chicken."

A slight lisp had turned into permanent slurring from decades of blackberry brandy and Southwest side blow.

He had a half-Mexican daughter, a Muslim son-in-law; the little man in fake gold that hung on the cross from the chain around his neck had been Jewish.

In the basement of his muffler shop, twenty white guys he thought were his friends bet fifty bucks he'd be too scared to pull the trigger.

He had to live to collect. He wouldn't.

Marquee de Sade

The office was on a farm, which seemed odd for a talent agent, but Samantha's best friend insisted she take Arielle to meet him.

Samantha's daughter had wanted to be an actress forever. At nine years old, Samantha felt she was ready.

The receptionist walked them down a hallway with multiple portraits of JFK and Lincoln.

Inside the suite was a massive fish tank. There were no visible fish, but two scale models:

The Titanic and The Edmund Fitzgerald.

The agent spun around on a chair, smiled at Arielle and said, "Are you ready for the glamorous world of failure?"

Chilly

Ike was pretty sure he had convinced Pellman to go into business with him.

Pellman had texted to say he had something delivered to Ike's office.

Ike drove up to his small office and freaked.

A refrigerator box with a ribbon blocked the door.

He called Pellman.

"I appreciate the new fridge, Pellman, though my old one works fine.

But the delivery idiot blocked the door with it."

Pellman grunted.

"We can't be partners, Ike. I put that box there this morning, by myself. It's empty. Wanted to see if you would try to move it or panic. You panicked."

Misspelling

Winthrop wrote her poetry and couldn't spell for shit.

She weighed it, earnestly and often.

I have a man who loves me and writes me poetry. For that, I'm lucky, but the mistakes, the uneducated nature of the poems make my glasses fog with disgust.

She knew she couldn't love him back enough. He would catch on and the poems would cease. She felt it.

She bought a small cedar box.

"Put the poems in here when you write them. Read them to me over the phone."

"There will be no more," Winthrop said, "My cousin was released from prison."

Volunteer

When his community service was completed, he had stayed. An anomaly.

Seven years, ten days sober, nearly seven volunteering at the food bank.

He walked home, past the scrapyard, where a man stood outside, catalytic converter in hand. No ordinary man, Larry knew, but The Beast. Won twenty-eight games in a season before high living became addiction.

Larry wanted to help, start with hello.

Larry shivered, cold and nervous. A hero of his who shared his affliction. The Beast's coffee cup was not just coffee, Larry knew.

The Beast offered. Larry couldn't say no to The Beast, and he gulped.

By Association

Jenny sang her ass off in the local round of Idol — nothing — never heard back from America's Got Talent. If you pause at the right moment, you can see her in line to audition for The Voice, and she even went to the Wheel of Fortune contestant search.

Fame eluded her.

Then she woke up ubiquitous on Twitter. Kind of, anyway, her arm around Nicky Arlon, in her horrible prom dress: the first picture of Nicky, leaked after he blew up a full school bus. Her face was pixelated to protect anonymity, an anonymity she immediately worked to dispense of.

Cinnamon Trick

Felix thought about the siren. They always silenced it leaving these things, out of respect for the neighbors.

But there was often a different wail. He wanted a cigarette.

"Twelve minutes, you get your cigarette," Amy whispered, knowing.

"It's a fucking cinnamon trick, Amy."

Amy slid the corpse inside the ambulance. The wailing mother, aunt, whoever, was pawing at her shoulder.

Amy got in the front. They rode off, siren silent.

"Cinnamon trick?" Amy asked.

"People trying to eat a spoonful of cinnamon. Everyone thought they could beat it. They can't. It fizzled out. Dope is the endless cinnamon trick."

Send Flowers

None of the flower arrangements were perfect, but Gail knew she had to send Hannah something; the death of Hannah's beloved eighteen-year-old cat was ripping her apart.

Gail finished typing the credit card info and hit the purchase tab, immediately remembering the day she told her parents that she was quitting vet school because she couldn't deal with the euthanasia, the sadness, the finality.

They were disappointed but supported her decision. They were encouraging when she went to journalism school, thrilled when she got her degree, and patiently listened to her complain when she got assigned to the obituary desk.

Cathedrals

The missionary, the papa, brought flat pieces of wood when he came to the island.

He showed Adama photos of cathedrals. With glue and a file, Adama made the wood look like the cathedrals. The missionary took them.

One day a woman came. She chose Adama and some classmates to live with her in the big cathedral country.

They went to movies and sporting events and to the curb to visit the ice cream truck.

They went to a gallery where Adama's cathedrals were on display.

The missionary had given Adama popsicle sticks but never once brought him a popsicle.

Frightening

An errant hunk of black marshmallow sizzled on a log.

Justin poked it with his stick and asked, "Know any scary stories, Uncle Geoff?"

Geoff sipped his whiskey and Vernor's out of a thermos and belched.

"I know a story about some stories."

"Tell me," his nephew said.

"Know how in scary stories kids are walking through the woods, terrified of the unknown, and they're thrilled to see a light in a cabin?"

Justin nodded.

"Them kids ever get eaten by a bear or a wolf?" Geoff asked.
"Hell no. People are the monsters. In the cabin and real life."

Higher Learning

Linda didn't feel like talking. It was the lobby of the DMV, not a damn party, but the woman next to her wasn't gonna let that stop her.

"I need to renew this. My son just got his Master's in finance. We're flying to Vermont. He was very successful, anyway: beautiful wife, but he felt he needed a better degree. You have kids?"

"Yeah," Linda said. "My kid rescued a squirrel caught in our gutter. Got rust in his eye. They had to remove his left eye. I'm getting my commercial license so I can take over his towing business."

Duck and Cover

There was a little scar on VanAllen's cheek that he could see in every photograph.

It was from his last fistfight, a snowy night in Quebec when his date butchered some French so badly that the guy outside the pool hall felt he was being mocked.

VanAllen could still see the silvery ring he wasn't quick enough to duck and feel the soft mush of his oversized gloves glancing the man's beard, harmlessly.

The consultation had been for surgery to mitigate the scar, but within an hour the aging lothario had agreed to a full facelift and a stronger jawline.

24 Hour Protection

Was dignity measured in how many of your life's breaths were taken with ease, at peace?

Bauer had never been certain how to measure dignity, but he knew that whatever the scale in question, his score on it was plummeting.

He'd show up at his sister's house unannounced. If he called, she'd know what it was about.

He pulled the tie she had gotten him for his birthday off the hanger and realized he had forgotten deodorant.

Popping the top, he could see the plastic holding a tiny veneer of the product. The last of his dignity scraped his armpits.

Dealey Plaza

I don't remember much, but I remember really wanting to climb a tree. Like tugging at my dad to take me to it. He would not.

I remember bending to pick up a rock and wanting to throw the rock, but too many grownups were nearby. They say now there was a grassy knoll, but all I saw were the asses and legs of the big people in front of me.

My mom squealed with excitement when she saw the convertible limo. My dad lifted me to his shoulders, then a loud noise; then he smothered me, shaking and angry.

Dark Flower Passion

Niko Cormier watched the last truck pull away, the sign with his great-grandpa's name inside it.

Without the sign lit, the street was dark, something he hadn't considered and would fix.

He called Naomi.

"It's done, my crazy flower."

"I'm proud of you, Niko. I know it wasn't easy."

"I got every last employee placed in a new gig. That made it easier."

"What now?" she asked.

"I think I'm gonna sit upstairs, draw the design for the roller derby track. Wanna join me?"

"I love your passion, Niko, but I'll wait until it stops smelling like a meatpacking plant.

Belle

Her thigh had a large spider vein. It caught my eye, but it didn't matter. I was looking at her thigh after years of lust and longing.

Technology, which I shunned, I now applauded for bringing us together.

We took a picnic to an island and found the most secluded spot we could.

Her feet dangled in muddy water. My tongue might as well have been severed from my body and my larynx stuffed with cotton.

We didn't get naked on that island. We soon would.

Her husband began to threaten me. He had no idea I would die happy.

Breakup

"...is a travesty." Travesty. She always mined her vocabulary for lofty words when she was angry. But when their conversations were about photography and surfing, she was the verbal ballerina of "for sures" and "totallys." He was convinced she hadn't noticed he was packing underwear. She was busy impressing herself with her speech—a speech that was supposed to bring about change in his behavior. She didn't bother to examine the clear evidence: he was leaving. The toothbrush should've made it real. Now he just needed his Xanax. Next to her elbow. Dammit. Bill would have some. He usually did.

Correspondence

Witzker was carving an eagle for George, the retired Marine, when squirrels chasing each other like motorcycle racers serpentined through his woodshop. Distracted, he took a hefty chunk out of his thumb.

Pulled a bandage from the drawer; slapped it on; finished the job.

Four beers and a shot after Witzker finished, he decided he'd write to Elizabeth. She'd blocked him on social media; snail mail was the only way.

Six bourbons later he weaved to the mailbox. Elizabeth needed to know his feelings.

All she knew when she saw the blood-stained envelope was that she was calling the cops.

Uniforms

Before the first asparagus was speared off a plate, Albert made a derogatory remark about Kellen's motorcycle club.

Her brother came out of the womb pompous, self-righteous.

"That gang's bringing drugs over the border, destroying the community," he said, lifting whiskey to his lips.

Olivia smirked.

"Cormorant Metals taking three thousand jobs to Singapore destroyed the community, Albert."

"Well, they're gone, and your son and his leather-clad thugs still roam."

"They're not perfect," Olivia said, "but your silk tie clad corporate heroes are more of a gang, only concerned with their wallets. At least the Switchblades run a toy drive."

First Kisses

In what would foreshadow decades, I kissed Don Q first, many times, as we shared a motionless dance by a man-made lake.

Then, in some twist on Pinocchio, a real, live person appeared out of the pulsing crowd from which I had escaped.

"Do you need a friend?" she asked. I suppose I gave her a seductive, delinquent shrug.

My breath must have smelled like high-octane fuel as she locked my lips and dove her tongue inward in a thrilling but graceless tango.

She'll never know she rescued me from feeling worthless and I wish I could tell her now.

Fresh Air

Kane saw the man every day during his jog. Today he cramped and slowed, reading the marker scrawl on cardboard.

Please help me feed my cats.

"Where do you keep your cats if you're homeless?" Kane asked.

"I'm not homeless, just jobless. I have a trailer home in Creekside, six blocks that way."

"How many cats do you have?"

"Fourteen," the man answered.

Kane pulled his emergency fifty from his sock.

"You're here all the time. Get some food; spend some time with your cats," he said.

The man scowled. "I can't sit home all day. Too many damn cats."

Lost

The tooth came loose when Brennan was dancing in the backyard. He shrieked with glee and ran inside.

Before Frank's wife had rinsed the blood off, he was describing the Tooth Fairy he imagined in vivid detail.

Frank grimaced. When Brennan turned to him, he smiled at his son weakly, a default.

Liz knew their son was gay. Liz knew her husband was not handling it well.

She hoped he would have a change of heart.

Liz could not wait to slip ten bucks under the pillow.

Frank could not wait to steal it and buy a pack of dope.

Revival

The dancefloor lights looked beautiful shining through the stained-glass windows out into the neighborhood.

Some of the old-timers went crazy that the church was now a popular nightclub.

Eddie had laughed at the quotes in the paper, the outrage.

Now he was working on the dancefloor, pumping, sweating.

The dancefloor that had once been an altar.

He pumped and sweated, grunted a bit.

His parents were married on this very altar.

He thought of his father, long gone, his mother in a home, and the college girl, who was OD'ing in this church, despite Eddie's best efforts to revive her.

Suburban Gospel

"I'm filing for divorce, Janelle."

Janelle closed the refrigerator door.

"You're going to end our marriage because you can't come to terms with my new relationship with Jesus Christ?"

"No," Daniel said, "I'm ending it because you gave twenty percent of our income to a guy who interprets a book for you out of a defunct movie theater."

"That's unfair."

"It's certainly not untrue."

"People change, Daniel."

Daniel lowered his voice.

"Yes, Janelle, people change. Some people go from liking Pearl Jam to liking Michael Buble. This is bigger than that, though I would probably divorce you over Buble too."

Close to Homeless

The tourists took pictures of the statue I had ignored.

They were startled by my presence, then my appearance.

They caught themselves and forced smiles. Maybe one was genuine, sympathetic.

To put them at ease I produced my camera.

The sun was at a perfect height in the sky, creating a halo behind the stone religious man.

I admired my photo and walked on.

Later, I let the tourists pass. A neighbor smiled and greeted them. I assume they smiled back.

He saw me. His smile dissolved. They were clean. I was dirty.

But I had taken a beautiful picture.

Impulsive

Niki was impulsive. She took pride in that, in being uncontainable and had great reflexes from her days as a gymnast.

Probably not a great idea to leap from her car while the other car's bumper was still airborne, but here she was, in the middle of the highway, surveying wreckage that wasn't done wrecking.

The woman in the other car was unconscious.

Niki realized the woman had crossed the center line.

Had she had a seizure?

The woman was bleeding. Her wrist. Both wrists.

The cuts were vertical and self inflicted.

Niki realized the woman had changed her mind.

Little Bomb

The sidewalk past the alley was littered with nitrous oxide cartridges, dozens of little bombs without a plane to load them on.

Jerry stepped over some, then *on* one, his ankle twisting slightly, his maternal profanity echoing down the empty city street.

He wondered how much kids paid for the damn things now; he wondered if their parents knew. He wondered how long the high of inhaling the balloon full of gas lasted.

Then he crossed the street, under the light, and realized he might remember how long the high lasted if years ago he hadn't gotten so high himself.

Inri   **Mattie Armstrong**

Innocence

She came from a different culture, but she loved their beautiful stone and glass building.

She was not sure about the words they spoke or the things they insisted were true.

She loved the melodies of their songs and sang along, even though she did not always understand.

She rejoiced in the voices that carried in unison, seeming to make the small red candles dance. Though she felt like an outsider, they welcomed her.

She thought she would never understand their beliefs and their rituals, but she knew, without a doubt, that those in power could torture an innocent man.

Inspred by the art of Mattie Armstrong

Callous

Braden was that afterthought guy, on the fringe of a group of friends.

Smaller of stature, he'd get shoved out of a heated argument or a raucous, drunken group hug. He began to think of himself as a callus. Uncomfortable, not quite painful.

Bob, Rick, Marty, all of 'em, they treated him the same. Rarely called for card games, last for sports tickets.

Then he caught the guy, the one assaulting college girls. In the right alley at the right time. Knocked him out.

Hero. The media swarmed.

Bob, Rick, Marty all told different reporters they were his best friend.

Happy

There was one clause in the contract he hated, one that very briefly made him consider saying no: he could not be identified in photos as the man who wore the Hank the Happy Hippopotamus costume.

Decades later, it was the best thing that ever happened to Will Rhinehart.

The final season premiere was at the Marshall Theater, and five thousand kids were going insane with laughter.

They didn't know it was him up there on the screen They didn't know that Hank the Happy Hippo was dying, and he was grateful that, anonymously, he would make kids laugh forever.

Catching Up

It was Deborah's idea to meet in a strip club.

Kind weirded Malcolm out. The few Facebook posts he'd seen were left-leaning, feminist.

Deb spoke first.

"Twenty-two years. Looks like your trip to Costa Rica to be a unicycle rider didn't work out."

Malcolm smiled.

"It was Peru to learn holistic dentistry, but it doesn't matter."

Deb smiled back.

"No, it doesn't, but the timing wasn't great."

Malcolm's smile faded.

"I thought we were gonna catch up. Why the strip club?"

Deborah guzzled her drink.

"Because the abortion you wouldn't pay for is the tall one in the red G-String."

Etched

His dad was more affectionate than usual. By a lot. They stood in the damp yard of the Memorial Granite place, waiting to see the family headstone.

"Your momma, she ordered this 'fore she passed."

The engraver unveiled the stone.

His mother, of course, who would lay beneath it this weekend.

His father's name engraved to the right of Mom.

Then his sister.

Then him. He shuddered. His mortality thrown at him like a Molotov.

And a name to the right. Same birthdate.

His dad spoke.

"We put your twin brother up for adoption.

Kept you. He'll be here tomorrow."

Dried Blood Icon

Engel never wanted to be a guy that bus drivers knew by name, but on some days their recognition seemed like all that he had.

The half pint in his breast pocket, above his heart, was all the security in the world.

He took a seat in the far back where he could nip at his eighty proof, emotional bubble wrap unperturbed.

Engel picked a scab at his temple from a fight. Yesterday? Maybe the day before. Maybe last week. The scab flaked off in his hand.

It was shaped like an angel, but Engel knew scabs couldn't save him.

Dust Jackets

They met at a book show in a Midwest farmer's market. Her historical fiction was leaving her table like they were bound with helium and he was in the corner, ignored, with his rehab chapbook and roll-your-owns.

She loved his wit; he loved her tits and her potential.

Now "they" were rich, and her next bestseller was drinking three bottles of Beaujolais.

It was like their addictions were on either side of a toll road. One had paid the fare; the other was at the booth extracting the entry ticket from the slot.

If only she could remember his book.

Visitor

On the farm, he'd been happy. No neighbors for miles.

But his future was in the city: a row of apartments, cramped, crowded.

HIs first night, his very first night, he saw a glimpse of a nude neighbor entering the shower.

A flash of buttock, nothing more.

He wasn't lonely on the farm.

The city bustled. It throbbed. He couldn't be lonely.

He posted at his window. Days later, another flash of nudity, a brief thrill, a connection.

On the street, he wondered... Which face belonged to the derriere?

He stayed in his window, watching, not knowing he was lonely.

Blind Date

She sat at a table, purposely facing the door.

He could see her and change his mind.

Don't touch the scar, she reminded herself.

"If he says something," Marla had told her, "tell him it's none of his fucking business."

She decided on, "I'd rather not talk about it."

The host sat him.

He had a beautiful smile. He was a brilliant conversationalist. Gave no hint that her windshield kissed face bothered him.

The scar never came up.

They drank wine at his opulent house, had great sex.

His first words at breakfast were "My brother is a cosmetic surgeon."

Better

He gave the street artist fifteen dollars for the sketch and told him that he was much better than the man with the huge gallery on St. Claude.

"Better?" the artist asked. "I'm glad you like my work, but he is "better." More people buy his work. He has a beautiful wife. They seem very much in love. I must assume he is not behind on his water bill."

The man tried to pay another ten for the sketch.

The artist declined.

"I don't need your pity. I just want you to know the definition of a truly common word."

Bookshelves

Three damn invitations and Ben's response to Lucy was the same:

"I'm building bookshelves."

The fourth invitation began, "If you're not building bookshelves, we're hitting Shelby's…"

"I am building bookshelves."

Lucy exhaled menthol smoke like it was truck exhaust.

"I wanna see these marvelous bookshelves soon."

And two months later, he invited her to see them.

It had not been a lie.

The shelves were magnificent, curled maple, expert crafting, exquisite.

Ben poured the drinks, Lucy stared at dog-eared word search books.

Only word search books.

Cans of pencils were the bookends.

No novels. No nonfiction. Not even a dictionary.

Branded

Clancy took the long way around because he always did. And he was always tempted not to.

His mom's storefront church was still a neighborhood landmark.

And, in Clancy's mind, a brutal, ridiculous cult.

A lucrative, brutal cult, that made his cousin a millionaire out of a former laundromat.

People had forgotten his mother started the charade until her recent death.

His name was included in the obituary, and the derision began again.

He braced himself as he walked into the deli to grab his sandwich.

The girl behind the counter smiled. Branded on her arm was the cult logo.

Code Violation

Tyler wheeled himself back from the table, telling his date a story he'd told hundreds of times.

"... I truly had no idea they were gonna do it. The Graystone was packed. They lifted me, threw me on stage in the middle of the encore. I landed, freaking out, totally disoriented."

"Excuse me," the man next to Tyler and Doreen said, "I'm a city attorney. Been trying to get that rattrap shut down forever. If you were injured…"

Tyler laughed angrily.

"Been in a chair since I can remember, asswipe. I wasn't injured. Stagediving was the greatest time of my life."

Heavens Above

Penny demanded and got a first-floor apartment.

She didn't worry about her vertigo.

She fed the squirrels.

She heard the thumps.

The first thump was Donna, her friend in the apartment directly above, who had told her it was the loveliest assisted living facility around.

Penny called the office.

"I think Donna fell."

Donna indeed had fallen. She wouldn't live above Penny again.

Frederick moved in next.

They played rummy, until one night, above her, she heard a thump.

She called.

No more cards with Frederick.

Penny lived a good life and was grateful her thump wouldn't upset anyone below.

Inspired by Mrs. Pat Kirchner

Next Year a Nativity

They met at FrostyWhip.

Steve insisted that he and Mark pose for their first Christmas picture in front of the giant swirled cone on the roof.

"It's not only romantic, it's the only kitschy landmark in this sleepy village."

Mark resisted.

"There's so much snow, you won't even be able to see the chocolate part. It will look vanilla. Or worse, like a Klan hood."

Steve got his way. They drove to FrostyWhip.

The high afternoon sun shone down. They found a passerby to snap a photo, just as the melting snow slid off the cone and knocked Steve unconscious.

Charmed

Velly was a "burn your mouth" guy. He'd pull pizza off the tray at Nimbo's, steam like bay fog coming off it, cheese like lava, and jam it in his face while the server was on the "beak" of be careful it's hot.

Cyrus needed the papers signed. Now Velly was meticulous, continental drift, agonizingly poring over the standard performance contract.

"I gotta catch that train, Velly."

 Velly topped off his coffee. Of course.

Cyrus got to the station. Train gone. Went to the bar. Train derailed. Four dead.

Cyrus texted Velly.

Velly replied, "I always know what I'm doing."

Flight Plan

It was career day. The hand hit his shoulder the same time the bad aftershave hit his nose.

"It's an outstanding illustration, Son. You have a bright future in the aerospace industry."

Marcus nodded, intent on finishing the tail.

He wondered now if the man's grandkids ever flew his designs. It had taken him a while before they were widely manufactured.

He watched with pride as the first one rolled off the line and took flight. Of course, he himself took it for a spin.

A shame his own dad wasn't there when he won Kite Designer of the Year.

Boiling Point

The argument raged inside Casey's so loudly you could hear it over the jukebox, in the ladies 'room, parking lot, everywhere.

Grease tried to ignore it but chimed in. This was gonna lead to violence. They all knew.

Grease was gonna walk away when Albie rushed him, then they were on the pool table, slugging.

Grease managed to grab a ball from underneath him and shattered Albie's cheekbone.

Casey himself put a gun to Grease's head.

Grease stood.

"Sorry, boss. This mean I'm fired?"

Casey chuckled. "No way. Back in the kitchen. I'd never find a better cook than you."

Church Organs

Gin and frozen mini tacos were battling for intestinal dominance. Lou was getting wobbly.

It would have been unpleasant at home, but he was currently at St. Josaphat, in line for communion.

Tonight was Christmas Eve; he had promised his mom he would attend mass. Now he was yards from the altar, sweating, shaking, clenching his cheeks.

He needed salvation from his own bowels, and it wasn't forthcoming.

Three people in front of him, Lou was Cardinal red in the face, about to soil himself.

He turned and sprinted down the aisle.

An elderly woman with a rosary screamed, "Heretic!"

Insurance

Sandra dreaded the call, but she had to let her mom know she was finally getting married.

Her mom answered. She very calmly said, "Carol and I have set a wedding date and though you refuse to meet her, we both want you to be there."

Sandra's mother answered as Sandra expected.

"The Lord and I only recognize a marriage between man and woman."

Sandra replied, "She's a wonderful person. I'm in love. You would love her. She's funny; she's got a great job with great benefits…"

"Health insurance?" her mom asked.

"Yes, Mother."

"What color dress should I wear?"

Battlefield

Marc was theorizing about the attractiveness of the late-night radio DJ when Devon jerked the car toward the curb.

A man on the sidewalk weaved in a serpentine, hunched, clutching an empty pint.

Devon hopped out.

"C'mon buddy, I'll give ya a ride wherever you're going."

They dropped him at the Hotel Yorba, Devon helping him to the door.

Marc stared at his friend as they drove off.

"That was reckless. You didn't know that guy. He coulda …"

Devon stared back.

"You don't know everyone on the battlefield with you by name, but you always assist a wounded soldier."

Highlights

The girls joked after the funeral that they were surprised their Dad hadn't asked to be buried in his high school football uniform.

It used to take him six beers to start the football stories; at the end they were constant.

They began to clean out his house when Sarah found the round canisters of sixteen millimeter film.

Natalie smiled "Football, I bet you."

They paid a post-production house to transfer them to DVD.

Waiting for sports, they got bondage. Dad and a blonde.

"Off. That's not Mom," Sarah muttered.

A busty brunette entered the screen.

Natalie said, "That is."

Liquid Courage

Nina Walcott smelled Wally first and told the teacher.

The city had shut off their water. His momma had gotten tired of him bathing with store-bought water.

He got taken aside and given a hygiene lecture he didn't need.

Wally thought of Nina as he read the email.

He could easily email back, but he got in his car, speeding to the accounting office.

"You own 620 units and in none of them are you legally obligated to provide water," Doyle said, repeating his email.

"My residential units come with water, or my new accountant search starts now," Wally answered.

Post-It-Note

I told her not to be specific on those little notes. She loves those. And never listens. The note doesn't have to say "Dr." I don't want Wren to think I got trouble. I only do crank with him. This one says "social worker". Wren might think it was just a girl. A pretty girl.

He's mad. "Social worker" could be a narc. "Mom! No more notes on the door!"

Wren's mad now. He flicks cigarette butts at me. Social worker. Narc. Same thing. Dammit. She's pretty. I wouldn't forget.

If I just would have gotten that sword for Christmas.

Schoolhouse Rock

Abe pulled the flap of paper off the flyer seeking "vocalist" and sent an email.

Zooey was the songwriter's name. She made it clear it was a get to know you session and not an audition.

A beer and a shot later, they were in her studio and it was an audition.

He loved her guitar melodies, and, though rusty, he was hitting the notes and really feeling like magic was happening.

She stopped midway through the third song.

"This isn't gonna work out."

Abe was shattered "But it seemed..."

"Sorry," she said, "but you mispronounced calliope, schadenfreude, and Kahlo."

Sanctuary

Old man Ferguson walked in, laboring more than usual.

The other girls snickered derisively while Shana helped him to his favorite booth.

Ferguson would stay for an hour and tip exactly a quarter.

Shana fell in love with the old guy because he wore his dog's ashes around his neck in a charm.

She told him how she was gonna open an elderly dog sanctuary one day. And he always said, "You will."

Tonight, he said, "I'm going to a rest home. Here."

The envelope contained the deed to 170 acres in Baraga County.

"Take good care of the doggies."

Art Credits

Action Figures "No Youth" by Sean Nader Instagram @SeanNader

Performance   "Untitled" by Bumbo Brian Krawczyk
                                Instagram @BumboKrawczyk

Extricated "Rainy Slushy NYC" by Andy Krieger www.andykriegerartist.com

Passionate "Saturday Chill" by John Bunkley www.johnbunkley.com

Witness   "Death and Texas" by Aimee Chorkey   Instagram @AimeeChorkey

Innocence "Inri" by Mattie Armstrong www.mattiearmstrongart.com

Prompts

Bears & Wolves	Three-word prompt from Daren Willacker
Man	Prompted by the editors of the Daily Drunk
The Bell and the Owl	Prompt from Katie Coon
Hunger Sun Fruit	Prompted by Megan Duhr-Vanelli
Fire, Water, Air	Prompted by Stacy Ferrington

Jimmy Doom is a writer and actor from Detroit, Michigan. He has gotten his ass kicked hundreds of times, both on camera and off. He currently resides in Hamtramck, Michigan with his cat, Stripper, and his liver, The Rock of Gibraltar.

Read more at www.jimmydoom.substack.com.

Made in the USA
Monee, IL
24 April 2021